A LONDON LIFE

by Henry James

GROVE PRESS · *New York*

A London Life is published in three editions:
An Evergreen Book (E-58)
A hard bound edition
A specially bound, Limited Edition of 100 numbered copies

Library of Congress Catalog Card Number 57-6531

Grove Press Books and Evergreen Books
are published by Barney Rosset

795 Broadway   *New York, N. Y.*

MANUFACTURED IN THE UNITED STATES OF AMERICA

A LONDON LIFE

I

IT was raining, apparently, but she didn't mind—
she would put on stout shoes and walk over to
Plash. She was restless and so fidgety that it was
a pain ; there were strange voices that frightened
her—they threw out the ugliest intimations—in the
empty rooms at home. She would see old Mrs.
Berrington, whom she liked because she was so
simple, and old Lady Davenant, who was staying
with her and who was interesting for reasons with
which simplicity had nothing to do. Then she would
come back to the children's tea—she liked even
better the last half-hour in the schoolroom, with the
bread and butter, the candles and the red fire, the
little spasms of confidence of Miss Steet the nursery-
governess, and the society of Scratch and Parson
(their nicknames would have made you think they
were dogs) her small, magnificent nephews, whose
flesh was so firm yet so soft and their eyes so
charming when they listened to stories. Plash was
the dower-house and about a mile and a half, through
the park, from Mellows. It was not raining after
all, though it had been ; there was only a grayness

in the air, covering all the strong, rich green, and a
pleasant damp, earthy smell, and the walks were
smooth and hard, so that the expedition was not
arduous.

The girl had been in England more than a year,
but there were some satisfactions she had not got
used to yet nor ceased to enjoy, and one of these
was the accessibility, the convenience of the country.
Within the lodge-gates or without them it seemed
all alike a park—it was all so intensely 'property.'
The very name of Plash, which was quaint and old,
had not lost its effect upon her, nor had it become
indifferent to her that the place was a dower-house
—the little red-walled, ivied asylum to which old
Mrs. Berrington had retired when, on his father's
death, her son came into the estates. Laura Wing
thought very ill of the custom of the expropriation
of the widow in the evening of her days, when honour
and abundance should attend her more than ever;
but her condemnation of this wrong forgot itself
when so many of the consequences looked right—bar-
ring a little dampness : which was the fate sooner or
later of most of her unfavourable judgments of
English institutions. Iniquities in such a country
somehow always made pictures ; and there had been
dower-houses in the novels, mainly of fashionable life,
on which her later childhood was fed. The iniquity
did not as a general thing prevent these retreats
from being occupied by old ladies with wonderful
reminiscences and rare voices, whose reverses had
not deprived them of a great deal of becoming
hereditary lace. In the park, half-way, suddenly,
Laura stopped, with a pain—a moral pang—that
almost took away her breath ; she looked at the

misty glades and the dear old beeches (so familiar
they were now and loved as much as if she owned
them); they seemed in their unlighted December
bareness conscious of all the trouble, and they made
her conscious of all the change. A year ago she
knew nothing, and now she knew almost everything ;
and the worst of her knowledge (or at least the
worst of the fears she had raised upon it) had come
to her in that beautiful place, where everything was
so full of peace and purity, of the air of happy submission to immemorial law. The place was the
same, but her eyes were different : they had seen
such sad, bad things in so short a time. Yes, the
time was short and everything was strange. Laura
Wing was too uneasy even to sigh, and as she
walked on she lightened her tread almost as if she
were going on tiptoe.

At Plash the house seemed to shine in the wet air
—the tone of the mottled red walls and the limited
but perfect lawn to be the work of an artist's
brush. Lady Davenant was in the drawing-room,
in a low chair by one of the windows, reading the
second volume of a novel. There was the same
look of crisp chintz, of fresh flowers wherever flowers
could be put, of a wall-paper that was in the bad
taste of years before, but had been kept so that no
more money should be spent, and was almost covered
over with amateurish drawings and superior engrav-
ings, framed in narrow gilt with large margins. The
room had its bright, durable, sociable air, the air
that Laura Wing liked in so many English things—
that of being meant for daily life, for long periods,
for uses of high decency. But more than ever to-
day was it incongruous that such an habitation, with

its chintzes and its British poets, its well-worn carpets
and domestic art—the whole aspect so unmeretricious
and sincere—should have to do with lives that were
not right. Of course however it had to do only
indirectly, and the wrong life was not old Mrs.
Berrington's nor yet Lady Davenant's. If Selina
and Selina's doings were not an implication of such
an interior any more than it was for them an expli-
cation, this was because she had come from so far
off, was a foreign element altogether. Yet it was
there she had found her occasion, all the influences
that had altered her so (her sister had a theory that
she was metamorphosed, that when she was young
she seemed born for innocence) if not at Plash
at least at Mellows, for the two places after all had
ever so much in common, and there were rooms at
the great house that looked remarkably like Mrs.
Berrington's parlour.

Lady Davenant always had a head-dress of a
peculiar style, original and appropriate—a sort of
white veil or cape which came in a point to the
place on her forehead where her smooth hair began
to show and then covered her shoulders. It was
always exquisitely fresh and was partly the reason
why she struck the girl rather as a fine portrait than
as a living person. And yet she was full of life, old
as she was, and had been made finer, sharper and
more delicate, by nearly eighty years of it. It was
the hand of a master that Laura seemed to see in
her face, the witty expression of which shone like a
lamp through the ground-glass of her good breeding;
nature was always an artist, but not so much of an
artist as that. Infinite knowledge the girl attributed
to her, and that was why she liked her a little fear-

fully. Lady Davenant was not as a general thing
fond of the young or of invalids ; but she made an
exception as regards youth for the little girl from
America, the sister of the daughter-in-law of her
dearest friend. She took an interest in Laura
partly perhaps to make up for the tepidity with
which she regarded Selina. At all events she had
assumed the general responsibility of providing her
with a husband. She pretended to care equally
little for persons suffering from other forms of misfortune, but she was capable of finding excuses for
them when they had been sufficiently to blame.
She expected a great deal of attention, always wore
gloves in the house and never had anything in her
hand but a book. She neither embroidered nor
wrote—only read and talked. She had no special
conversation for girls but generally addressed them
in the same manner that she found effective with
her contemporaries. Laura Wing regarded this as
an honour, but very often she didn't know what the
old lady meant and was ashamed to ask her. Once
in a while Lady Davenant was ashamed to tell.
Mrs. Berrington had gone to a cottage to see an old
woman who was ill—an old woman who had been
in her service for years, in the old days. Unlike
her friend she was fond of young people and invalids,
but she was less interesting to Laura, except that it
was a sort of fascination to wonder how she could
have such abysses of placidity. She had long cheeks
and kind eyes and was devoted to birds ; somehow
she always made Laura think secretly of a tablet of
fine white soap—nothing else was so smooth and
clean.

‘And what's going on *chez vous*—who is there

and what are they doing?' Lady Davenant asked, after the first greetings.

'There isn't any one but me—and the children—and the governess.'

'What, no party—no private theatricals? How do you live?'

'Oh, it doesn't take so much to keep me going,' said Laura. 'I believe there were some people coming on Saturday, but they have been put off, or they can't come. Selina has gone to London.'

'And what has she gone to London for?'

'Oh, I don't know—she has so many things to do.'

'And where is Mr. Berrington?'

'He has been away somewhere; but I believe he is coming back to-morrow—or next day.'

'Or the day after?' said Lady Davenant. 'And do they never go away together?' she continued after a pause.

'Yes, sometimes—but they don't come back together.'

'Do you mean they quarrel on the way?'

'I don't know what they do, Lady Davenant—I don't understand,' Laura Wing replied, with an unguarded tremor in her voice. 'I don't think they are very happy.'

'Then they ought to be ashamed of themselves. They have got everything so comfortable—what more do they want?'

'Yes, and the children are such dears!'

'Certainly — charming. And is she a good person, the present governess? Does she look after them properly?'

'Yes—she seems very good—it's a blessing. But I think she's unhappy too.'

'Bless us, what a house! Does she want some one to make love to her?'

'No, but she wants Selina to see—to appreciate,' said the young girl.

'And doesn't she appreciate—when she leaves them that way quite to the young woman?'

'Miss Steet thinks she doesn't notice how they come on—she is never there.'

'And has she wept and told you so? You know they are always crying, governesses—whatever line you take. You shouldn't draw them out too much —they are always looking for a chance. She ought to be thankful to be let alone. You mustn't be too sympathetic—it's mostly wasted,' the old lady went on.

'Oh, I'm not—I assure you I'm not,' said Laura Wing. 'On the contrary, I see so much about me that I don't sympathise with.'

'Well, you mustn't be an impertinent little American either!' her interlocutress exclaimed. Laura sat with her for half an hour and the conversation took a turn through the affairs of Plash and through Lady Davenant's own, which were visits in prospect and ideas suggested more or less directly by them as well as by the books she had been reading, a heterogeneous pile on a table near her, all of them new and clean, from a circulating library in London. The old woman had ideas and Laura liked them, though they often struck her as very sharp and hard, because at Mellows she had no diet of that sort. There had never been an idea in the house, since she came at least, and there was wonderfully little reading. Lady Davenant still went from country-house to country-house all winter,

as she had done all her life, and when Laura asked
her she told her the places and the people she
probably should find at each of them.   Such an
enumeration was much less interesting to the
girl than it would have been a year before : she
herself had now seen a great many places and
people and the freshness of her curiosity was gone.
But she still cared for Lady Davenant's descriptions
and judgments, because they were the thing in her
life which (when she met the old woman from time
to time) most represented talk—the rare sort of talk
that was not mere chaff.   That was what she had
dreamed of before she came to England, but in
Selina's set the dream had not come true.   In
Selina's set people only harried each other from
morning till night with extravagant accusations—
it was all a kind of horse-play of false charges.
When Lady Davenant was accusatory it was within
the limits of perfect verisimilitude.

Laura waited for Mrs. Berrington to come in but
she failed to appear, so that the girl gathered her
waterproof together with an intention of departure.
But she was secretly reluctant, because she had
walked over to Plash with a vague hope that some
soothing hand would be laid upon her pain.   If
there was no comfort at the dower-house she knew
not where to look for it, for there was certainly none
at home—not even with Miss Steet and the children.
It was not Lady Davenant's leading characteristic
that she was comforting, and Laura had not aspired
to be coaxed or coddled into forgetfulness : she
wanted rather to be taught a certain fortitude— how
to live and hold up one's head even while knowing
that things were very bad.   A brazen indifference—

it was not exactly that that she wished to acquire ;
but were there not some sorts of indifference that
were philosophic and noble ? Could Lady Davenant
not teach them, if she should take the trouble ? The
girl remembered to have heard that there had been
years before some disagreeable occurrences in *her*
family ; it was not a race in which the ladies in-
veterately turned out well. Yet who to-day had the
stamp of honour and credit—of a past which was
either no one's business or was part and parcel of
a fair public record—and carried it so much as a
matter of course ? She herself had been a good
woman and that was the only thing that told in the
long run. It was Laura's own idea to be a good
woman and that this would make it an advantage
for Lady Davenant to show her how not to feel too
much. As regards feeling enough, that was a branch
in which she had no need to take lessons.

The old woman liked cutting new books, a task
she never remitted to her maid, and while her young
visitor sat there she went through the greater part
of a volume with the paper-knife. She didn't pro-
ceed very fast—there was a kind of patient, awkward
fumbling of her aged hands ; but as she passed her
knife into the last leaf she said abruptly—' And how
is your sister going on ? She's very light ! ' Lady
Davenant added before Laura had time to reply.

' Oh, Lady Davenant ! ' the girl exclaimed,
vaguely, slowly, vexed with herself as soon as she had
spoken for having uttered the words as a protest,
whereas she wished to draw her companion out. To
correct this impression she threw back her waterproof.

' Have you ever spoken to her ? ' the old woman
asked.

'Spoken to her?'

'About her behaviour.   I daresay you haven't—
you Americans have such a lot of false delicacy.   I
daresay Selina wouldn't speak to you if you were in
her place (excuse the supposition!) and yet she is
capable——'   But Lady Davenant paused, prefer-
ring not to say of what young Mrs. Berrington was
capable.   'It's a bad house for a girl.'

'It only gives me a horror,' said Laura, pausing
in turn.

'A horror of your sister?   That's not what one
should aim at.   You ought to get married—and the
sooner the better.   My dear child, I have neglected
you dreadfully.'

'I am much obliged to you, but if you think
marriage looks to me happy!' the girl exclaimed,
laughing without hilarity.

'Make it happy for some one else and you will
be happy enough yourself.   You ought to get out
of your situation.'

Laura Wing was silent a moment, though this
was not a new reflection to her.   'Do you mean
that I should leave Selina altogether?   I feel as
if I should abandon her—as if I should be a coward.'

'Oh, my dear, it isn't the business of little girls
to serve as parachutes to fly-away wives!   That's
why if you haven't spoken to her you needn't take
the trouble at this time of day.   Let her go—let
her go!'

'Let her go?' Laura repeated, staring.

Her companion gave her a sharper glance.   'Let
her stay, then!   Only get out of the house.   You
can come to me, you know, whenever you like.   I
don't know another girl I would say that to.'

'Oh, Lady Davenant,' Laura began again, but she only got as far as this; in a moment she had covered her face with her hands—she had burst into tears.

'Ah my dear, don't cry or I shall take back my invitation! It would never do if you were to *larmoyer.* If I have offended you by the way I have spoken of Selina I think you are too sensitive. We shouldn't feel more for people than they feel for themselves. She has no tears, I'm sure.'

'Oh, she has, she has!' cried the girl, sobbing with an odd effect as she put forth this pretension for her sister.

'Then she's worse than I thought. I don't mind them so much when they are merry but I hate them when they are sentimental.'

'She's so changed—so changed!' Laura Wing went on.

'Never, never, my dear: *c'est de naissance.*'

'You never knew my mother,' returned the girl; 'when I think of mother——' The words failed her while she sobbed.

'I daresay she was very nice,' said Lady Davenant gently. 'It would take that to account for you: such women as Selina are always easily enough accounted for. I didn't mean it was inherited— for that sort of thing skips about. I daresay there was some improper ancestress — except that you Americans don't seem to have ancestresses.'

Laura gave no sign of having heard these observations; she was occupied in brushing away her tears. 'Everything is so changed—you don't know,' she remarked in a moment. 'Nothing could have been happier — nothing could have been sweeter.

And now to be so dependent — so helpless — so poor!'

'Have you nothing at all?' asked Lady Davenant, with simplicity.

'Only enough to pay for my clothes.'

'That's a good deal, for a girl. You are uncommonly dressy, you know.'

'I'm sorry I seem so. That's just the way I don't want to look.'

'You Americans can't help it; you "wear" your very features and your eyes look as if they had just been sent home. But I confess you are not so smart as Selina.'

'Yes, isn't she splendid?' Laura exclaimed, with proud inconsequence. 'And the worse she is the better she looks.'

'Oh my child, if the bad women looked as bad as they are——! It's only the good ones who can afford that,' the old lady murmured.

'It was the last thing I ever thought of—that I should be ashamed,' said Laura.

'Oh, keep your shame till you have more to do with it. It's like lending your umbrella—when you have only one.'

'If anything were to happen—publicly—I should die, I·should die!' the girl exclaimed passionately and with a motion that carried her to her feet. This time she settled herself for departure. Lady Davenant's admonition rather frightened than sustained her.

The old woman leaned back in her chair, looking up at her. 'It would be very bad, I daresay. But it wouldn't prevent me from taking you in.'

Laura Wing returned her look, with eyes slightly

distended, musing. 'Think of having to come to that!'

Lady Davenant burst out laughing. 'Yes, yes, you must come; you are so original!'

'I don't mean that I don't feel your kindness,' the girl broke out, blushing. 'But to be only protected—always protected: is that a life?'

'Most women are only too thankful and I am bound to say I think you are *difficile.*' Lady Davenant used a good many French words, in the old-fashioned manner and with a pronunciation not perfectly pure: when she did so she reminded Laura Wing of Mrs. Gore's novels. 'But you shall be better protected than even by me. *Nous verrons cela.* Only you must stop crying—this isn't a crying country.'

'No, one must have courage here. It takes courage to marry for such a reason.'

'Any reason is good enough that keeps a woman from being an old maid. Besides, you will like him.'

'He must like me first,' said the girl, with a sad smile.

'There's the American again! It isn't necessary. You are too proud—you expect too much.'

'I'm proud for what I am—that's very certain. But I don't expect anything,' Laura Wing declared. 'That's the only form my pride takes. Please give my love to Mrs. Berrington. I am so sorry—so sorry,' she went on, to change the talk from the subject of her marrying. She wanted to marry but she wanted also not to want it and, above all, not to appear to. She lingered in the room, moving about a little; the place was always so pleasant to her that to go away—to return to her own barren home—

had the effect of forfeiting a sort of privilege of sanctuary. The afternoon had faded but the lamps had been brought in, the smell of flowers was in the air and the old house of Plash seemed to recognise the hour that suited it best. The quiet old lady in the firelight, encompassed with the symbolic security of chintz and water-colour, gave her a sudden vision of how blessed it would be to jump all the middle dangers of life and have arrived at the end, safely, sensibly, with a cap and gloves and consideration and memories. 'And, Lady Davenant, what does *she* think?' she asked abruptly, stopping short and referring to Mrs. Berrington.

'Think? Bless your soul, she doesn't do that! If she did, the things she says would be unpardonable.'

'The things she says?'

'That's what makes them so beautiful—that they are not spoiled by preparation. You could never think of them *for* her.' The girl smiled at this description of the dearest friend of her interlocutress, but she wondered a little what Lady Davenant would say to visitors about *her* if she should accept a refuge under her roof. Her speech was after all a flattering proof of confidence. 'She wishes it had been you—I happen to know that,' said the old woman.

'It had been me?'

'That Lionel had taken a fancy to.'

'I wouldn't have married him,' Laura rejoined, after a moment.

'Don't say that or you will make me think it won't be easy to help you. I shall depend upon you not to refuse anything so good.'

'I don't call him good. If he were good his wife would be better.'

'Very likely; and if you had married him *he*
would be better, and that's more to the purpose.
Lionel is as idiotic as a comic song, but you have
cleverness for two.'

'And you have it for fifty, dear Lady Davenant.
Never, never—I shall never marry a man I can't
respect!' Laura Wing exclaimed.

She had come a little nearer her old friend and
taken her hand; her companion held her a moment
and with the other hand pushed aside one of the
flaps of the waterproof.   'And what is it your cloth-
ing costs you?' asked Lady Davenant, looking at
the dress underneath and not giving any heed to
this declaration.

'I don't exactly know: it takes almost everything
that is sent me from America.   But that is dreadfully little—only a few pounds.   I am a wonderful
manager.   Besides,' the girl added, 'Selina wants
one to be dressed.'

'And doesn't she pay any of your bills?'

'Why, she gives me everything—food, shelter,
carriages.'

'Does she never give you money?'

'I wouldn't take it,' said the girl.   'They need
everything they have — their life is tremendously
expensive.'

'That I'll warrant!' cried the old woman.   'It
was a most beautiful property, but I don't know
what has become of it now.   *Ce n'est pas pour vous
blesser*, but the hole you Americans *can* make——'

Laura interrupted immediately, holding up her
head; Lady Davenant had dropped her hand and she
had receded a step.   'Selina brought Lionel a very
considerable fortune and every penny of it was paid.'

'Yes, I know it was ; Mrs. Berrington told me it was most satisfactory. That's not always the case with the fortunes you young ladies are supposed to bring!' the old lady added, smiling.

The girl looked over her head a moment. 'Why do your men marry for money?'

'Why indeed, my dear? And before your troubles what used your father to give you for your personal expenses?'

'He gave us everything we asked—we had no particular allowance.'

'And I daresay you asked for everything?' said Lady Davenant.

'No doubt we were very dressy, as you say.'

'No wonder he went bankrupt — for he did, didn't he?'

'He had dreadful reverses but he only sacrificed himself—he protected others.'

'Well, I know nothing about these things and I only ask *pour me renseigner*,' Mrs. Berrington's guest went on. 'And after their reverses your father and mother lived I think only a short time?'

Laura Wing had covered herself again with her mantle ; her eyes were now bent upon the ground and, standing there before her companion with her umbrella and her air of momentary submission and self-control, she might very well have been a young person in reduced circumstances applying for a place. 'It was short enough but it seemed—some parts of it—terribly long and painful. My poor father— my dear father,' the girl went on. But her voice trembled and she checked herself.

'I feel as if I were cross-questioning you, which God forbid!' said Lady Davenant. 'But there is one thing I should really like to know. Did Lionel and his wife, when you were poor, come freely to your assistance?'

'They sent us money repeatedly — it was *her* money of course. It was almost all we had.'

'And if you have been poor and know what poverty is tell me this : has it made you afraid to marry a poor man?'

It seemed to Lady Davenant that in answer to this her young friend looked at her strangely; and then the old woman heard her say something that had not quite the heroic ring she expected. 'I am afraid of so many things to-day that I don't know where my fears end.'

'I have no patience with the highstrung way you take things. But I have to know, you know.'

'Oh, don't try to know any more shames—any more horrors!' the girl wailed with sudden passion, turning away.

Her companion got up, drew her round again and kissed her. 'I think you would fidget me,' she remarked as she released her. Then, as if this were too cheerless a leave-taking, she added in a gayer tone, as Laura had her hand on the door : 'Mind what I tell you, my dear ; let her go !' It was to this that the girl's lesson in philosophy reduced itself, she reflected, as she walked back to Mellows in the rain, which had now come on, through the darkening park.

II

THE children were still at tea and poor Miss Steet
sat between them, consoling herself with strong cups,
crunching melancholy morsels of toast and dropping
an absent gaze on her little companions as they exchanged small, loud remarks.   She always sighed
when Laura came in—it was her way of expressing
appreciation of the visit—and she was the one person whom the girl frequently saw who seemed to her
more unhappy than herself.   But Laura envied her
—she thought her position had more dignity than
that of her employer's dependent sister.   Miss Steet
had related her life to the children's pretty young
aunt and this personage knew that though it had
had painful elements nothing so disagreeable had
ever befallen her or was likely to befall her as the
odious possibility of her sister's making a scandal.
She had two sisters (Laura knew all about them)
and one of them was married to a clergyman in
Staffordshire (a very ugly part) and had seven
children and four hundred a year; while the other,
the eldest, was enormously stout and filled (it was a
good deal of a squeeze) a position as matron in an
orphanage at Liverpool.   Neither of them seemed
destined to go into the English divorce-court, and

such a circumstance on the part of one's near relations struck Laura as in itself almost sufficient to
constitute happiness. Miss Steet never lived in a
state of nervous anxiety—everything about her was
respectable. She made the girl almost angry sometimes, by her drooping, martyr-like air : Laura was
near breaking out at her with, ' Dear me, what have
you got to complain of ? Don't you earn your living
like an honest girl and are you obliged to see things
going on about you that you hate ?'

But she could not say things like that to her,
because she had promised Selina, who made a great
point of this, that she would never be too familiar
with her. Selina was not without her ideas of
decorum—very far from it indeed ; only she erected
them in such queer places. She was not familiar
with her children's governess ; she was not even
familiar with the children themselves. That was
why after all it was impossible to address much of a
remonstrance to Miss Steet when she sat as if she
were tied to the stake and the fagots were being
lighted. If martyrs in this situation had tea and
cold meat served them they would strikingly have
resembled the provoking young woman in the schoolroom at Mellows. Laura could not have denied that
it was natural she should have liked it better if Mrs.
Berrington would *sometimes* just look in and give a
sign that she was pleased with her system ; but poor
Miss Steet only knew by the servants or by Laura
whether Mrs. Berrington were at home or not : she
was for the most part not, and the governess had a
way of silently intimating (it was the manner she put
her head on one side when she looked at Scratch and
Parson—of course *she* called them Geordie and Ferdy)

that she was immensely handicapped and even that
they were. Perhaps they were, though they certainly
showed it little in their appearance and manner, and
Laura was at least sure that if Selina had been perpetually dropping in Miss Steet would have taken
that discomfort even more tragically. The sight of
this young woman's either real or fancied wrongs did
not diminish her conviction that she herself would
have found courage to become a governess. She
would have had to teach very young children, for
she believed she was too ignorant for higher flights.
But Selina would never have consented to that—she
would have considered it a disgrace or even worse—
a *pose*. Laura had proposed to her six months
before that she should dispense with a paid governess
and suffer *her* to take charge of the little boys: in
that way she should not feel so completely dependent—she should be doing something in return.
'And pray what would happen when you came to
dinner? Who would look after them then?' Mrs.
Berrington had demanded, with a very shocked air.
Laura had replied that perhaps it was not absolutely
necessary that she should come to dinner—she could
dine early, with the children; and that if her presence
in the drawing-room should be required the children
had their nurse—and what did they have their nurse
for? Selina looked at her as if she was deplorably
superficial and told her that they had their nurse to
dress them and look after their clothes—did she
wish the poor little ducks to go in rags? She had
her own ideas of thoroughness and when Laura
hinted that after all at that hour the children
were in bed she declared that even when they were
asleep she desired the governess to be at hand—that

was the way a mother felt who really took an interest. Selina was wonderfully thorough ; she said something about the evening hours in the quiet schoolroom being the proper time for the governess to 'get up' the children's lessons for the next day. Laura Wing was conscious of her own ignorance ; nevertheless she presumed to believe that she could have taught Geordie and Ferdy the alphabet without anticipatory nocturnal researches. She wondered what her sister supposed Miss Steet taught them —whether she had a cheap theory that they were in Latin and algebra.

The governess's evening hours in the quiet school-room would have suited Laura well—so at least she believed ; by touches of her own she would make the place even prettier than it was already, and in the winter nights, near the bright fire, she would get through a delightful course of reading. There was the question of a new piano (the old one was pretty bad—Miss Steet had a finger !) and perhaps she should have to ask Selina for that—but it would be all. The schoolroom at Mellows was not a charm-less place and the girl often wished that she might have spent her own early years in so dear a scene. It was a sort of panelled parlour, in a wing, and looked out on the great cushiony lawns and a part of the terrace where the peacocks used most to spread their tails. There were quaint old maps on the wall, and ' collections '—birds and shells—under glass cases, and there was a wonderful pictured screen which old Mrs. Berrington had made when Lionel was young out of primitive woodcuts illustrative of nursery-tales. The place was a setting for rosy childhood, and Laura believed her sister never knew

how delightful Scratch and Parson looked there.
Old Mrs. Berrington had known in the case of
Lionel—it had all been arranged for him. That
was the story told by ever so many other things in
the house, which betrayed the full perception of a
comfortable, liberal, deeply domestic effect, addressed
to eternities of possession, characteristic thirty years
before of the unquestioned and unquestioning old
lady whose sofas and ' corners ' (she had perhaps been
the first person in England to have corners) demon-
strated the most of her cleverness.

Laura Wing envied English children, the boys at
least, and even her own chubby nephews, in spite
of the cloud that hung over them ; but she had
already noted the incongruity that appeared to-day
between Lionel Berrington at thirty-five and the
influences that had surrounded his younger years.
She did not dislike her brother-in-law, though she
admired him scantily, and she pitied him ; but she
marvelled at the waste involved in some human
institutions (the English country gentry for instance)
when she perceived that it had taken so much to
produce so little. The sweet old wainscoted parlour,
the view of the garden that reminded her of scenes
in Shakespeare's comedies, all that was exquisite in
the home of his forefathers—what visible reference
was there to these fine things in poor Lionel's stable-
stamped composition ? When she came in this
evening and saw his small sons making competitive
noises in their mugs (Miss Steet checked this impropriety on her entrance) she asked herself what
they would have to show twenty years later for the
frame that made them just then a picture. Would
they be wonderfully ripe and noble, the perfection of

human culture? The contrast was before her again, the sense of the same curious duplicity (in the literal meaning of the word) that she had felt at Plash— the way the genius of such an old house was all peace and decorum and the spirit that prevailed there, outside of the schoolroom, was contentious and impure. She had often been struck with it before—with that perfection of machinery which can still at certain times make English life go on of itself with a stately rhythm long after there is corruption within it.

She had half a purpose of asking Miss Steet to dine with her that evening downstairs, so absurd did it seem to her that two young women who had so much in common (enough at least for that) should sit feeding alone at opposite ends of the big empty house, melancholy on such a night. She would not have cared just now whether Selina did think such a course familiar: she indulged sometimes in a kind of angry humility, placing herself near to those who were laborious and sordid. But when she observed how much cold meat the governess had already consumed she felt that it would be a vain form to propose to her another repast. She sat down with her and presently, in the firelight, the two children had placed themselves in position for a story. They were dressed like the mariners of England and they smelt of the ablutions to which they had been condemned before tea and the odour of which was but partly overlaid by that of bread and butter. Scratch wanted an old story and Parson a new, and they exchanged from side to side a good many powerful arguments. While they were so engaged Miss Steet narrated at her visitor's invitation the walk she had

taken with them and revealed that she had been
thinking for a long time of asking Mrs. Berrington
—if she only had an opportunity—whether she
should approve of her giving them a few elementary
notions of botany. But the opportunity had not
come—she had had the idea for a long time past.
She was rather fond of the study herself; she had
gone into it a little—she seemed to intimate that
there had been times when she extracted a needed
comfort from it. Laura suggested that botany
might be a little dry for such young children in
winter, from text-books—that the better way would
be perhaps to wait till the spring and show them
out of doors, in the garden, some of the peculiarities
of plants. To this Miss Steet rejoined that her idea
had been to teach some of the general facts slowly
—it would take a long time—and then they would
be all ready for the spring. She spoke of the spring
as if it would not arrive for a terribly long time.
She had hoped to lay the question before Mrs.
Berrington that week—but was it not already
Thursday? Laura said, 'Oh yes, you had better
do anything with the children that will keep them
profitably occupied;' she came very near saying
anything that would occupy the governess herself.

She had rather a dread of new stories—it took
the little boys so long to get initiated and the first
steps were so terribly bestrewn with questions.
Receptive silence, broken only by an occasional
rectification on the part of the listener, never descended until after the tale had been told a dozen
times. The matter was settled for 'Riquet with the
Tuft,' but on this occasion the girl's heart was not

much in the entertainment. The children stood on either side of her, leaning against her, and she had an arm round each ; their little bodies were thick and strong and their voices had the quality of silver bells. Their mother had certainly gone too far ; but there was nevertheless a limit to the tenderness one could feel for the neglected, compromised bairns. It was difficult to take a sentimental view of them —they would never take such a view of themselves. Geordie would grow up to be a master-hand at polo and care more for that pastime than for anything in life, and Ferdy perhaps would develop into 'the best shot in England.' Laura felt these possibilities stirring within them ; they were in the things they said to her, in the things they said to each other. At any rate they would never reflect upon anything in the world. They contradicted each other on a question of ancestral history to which their attention apparently had been drawn by their nurse, whose people had been tenants for generations. Their grandfather had had the hounds for fifteen years— Ferdy maintained that he had always had them. Geordie ridiculed this idea, like a man of the world ; he had had them till he went into volunteering— then he had got up a magnificent regiment, he had spent thousands of pounds on it. Ferdy was of the opinion that this was wasted money—he himself intended to have a real regiment, to be a colonel in the Guards. Geordie looked as if he thought that a superficial ambition and could see beyond it ; his own most definite view was that he would have back the hounds. He didn't see why papa didn't have them—unless it was because he wouldn't take the trouble.

'I know—it's because mamma is an American!'
Ferdy announced, with confidence.

'And what has that to do with it?' asked Laura.

'Mamma spends so much money—there isn't any
more for anything!'

This startling speech elicited an alarmed protest
from Miss Steet; she blushed and assured Laura that
she couldn't imagine where the child could have picked
up such an extraordinary idea. 'I'll look into it—
you may be sure I'll look into it,' she said; while
Laura told Ferdy that he must never, never, never,
under any circumstances, either utter or listen to a
word that should be wanting in respect to his mother.

'If any one should say anything against any
of my people I would give him a good one!'
Geordie shouted, with his hands in his little blue
pockets.

'I'd hit him in the eye!' cried Ferdy, with
cheerful inconsequence.

'Perhaps you don't care to come to dinner at
half-past seven,' the girl said to Miss Steet; 'but I
should be very glad—I'm all alone.'

'Thank you so much. All alone, really?' murmured the governess.

'Why don't you get married? then you wouldn't
be alone,' Geordie interposed, with ingenuity.

'Children, you are really too dreadful this evening!' Miss Steet exclaimed.

'I shan't get married—I want to have the
hounds,' proclaimed Geordie, who had apparently
been much struck with his brother's explanation.

'I will come down afterwards, about half-past
eight, if you will allow me,' said Miss Steet, looking
conscious and responsible.

'Very well—perhaps we can have some music; we will try something together.'

'Oh, music—*we* don't go in for music!' said Geordie, with clear superiority; and while he spoke Laura saw Miss Steet get up suddenly, looking even less alleviated than usual. The door of the room had been pushed open and Lionel Berrington stood there. He had his hat on and a cigar in his mouth and his face was red, which was its common condition. He took off his hat as he came into the room, but he did not stop smoking and he turned a little redder than before. There were several ways in which his sister-in-law often wished he had been very different, but she had never disliked him for a certain boyish shyness that was in him, which came out in his dealings with almost all women. The governess of his children made him uncomfortable and Laura had already noticed that he had the same effect upon Miss Steet. He was fond of his children, but he saw them hardly more frequently than their mother and they never knew whether he were at home or away. Indeed his goings and comings were so frequent that Laura herself scarcely knew: it was an accident that on this occasion his absence had been marked for her. Selina had had her reasons for wishing not to go up to town while her husband was still at Mellows, and she cherished the irritating belief that he stayed at home on purpose to watch her—to keep her from going away. It was her theory that she herself was perpetually at home—that few women were more domestic, more glued to the fireside and absorbed in the duties belonging to it; and unreasonable as she was she recognised the fact that for her to

establish this theory she must make her husband
sometimes see her at Mellows. It was not enough
for her to maintain that he would see her if he
were sometimes there himself. Therefore she disliked to be caught in the crude fact of absence—to
go away under his nose ; what she preferred was to
take the next train after his own and return an hour
or two before him. She managed this often with
great ability, in spite of her not being able to be sure
when he *would* return. Of late however she had
ceased to take so much trouble, and Laura, by no
desire of the girl's own, was enough in the confidence of her impatiences and perversities to know
that for her to have wished (four days before the
moment I write of) to put him on a wrong scent—
or to keep him at least off the right one—she must
have had something more dreadful than usual in her
head. This was why the girl had been so nervous
and why the sense of an impending catastrophe,
which had lately gathered strength in her mind, was
at present almost intolerably pressing : she knew
how little Selina could afford to be more dreadful
than usual.

Lionel startled her by turning up in that unexpected way, though she could not have told herself
when it would have been natural to expect him.
This attitude, at Mellows, was left to the servants,
most of them inscrutable and incommunicative and
erect in a wisdom that was founded upon telegrams
—you couldn't speak to the butler but he pulled one
out of his pocket. It was a house of telegrams ;
they crossed each other a dozen times an hour,
coming and going, and Selina in particular lived in
a cloud of them. Laura had but vague ideas as to

what they were all about ; once in a while, when
they fell under her eyes, she either failed to understand them or judged them to be about horses.
There were an immense number of horses, in one
way and another, in Mrs. Berrington's life. Then
she had so many friends, who were always rushing
about like herself and making appointments and
putting them off and wanting to know if she were
going to certain places or whether she would go if they
did or whether she would come up to town and dine
and 'do a theatre.' There were also a good many
theatres in the existence of this busy lady. Laura
remembered how fond their poor father had been of
telegraphing, but it was never about the theatre : at
all events she tried to give her sister the benefit or
the excuse of heredity. Selina had her own opinions,
which were superior to this she once remarked to
Laura that it was idiotic for a woman to write—to
telegraph was the only way not to get into trouble.
If doing so sufficed to keep a lady out of it Mrs.
Berrington's life should have flowed like the rivers of
Eden.

III

LAURA, as soon as her brother-in-law had been in
the room a moment, had a particular fear; she had
seen him twice noticeably under the influence of
liquor; she had not liked it at all and now there
were some of the same signs. She was afraid the
children would discover them, or at any rate Miss
Steet, and she felt the importance of not letting him
stay in the room. She thought it almost a sign
that he should have come there at all—he was so
rare an apparition. He looked at her very hard,
smiling as if to say, 'No, no, I'm not—not if you
think it!' She perceived with relief in a moment
that he was not very bad, and liquor disposed him
apparently to tenderness, for he indulged in an
interminable kissing of Geordie and Ferdy, during
which Miss Steet turned away delicately, looking
out of the window. The little boys asked him no
questions to celebrate his return—they only announced that they were going to learn botany, to
which he replied: 'Are you, really? Why, I never
did,' and looked askance at the governess, blushing
as if to express the hope that she would let him off
from carrying that subject further. To Laura and
to Miss Steet he was amiably explanatory, though

his explanations were not quite coherent. He had
come back an hour before—he was going to spend
the night—he had driven over from Churton—he
was thinking of taking the last train up to town.
Was Laura dining at home? Was any one coming?
He should enjoy a quiet dinner awfully.

'Certainly I'm alone,' said the girl. 'I suppose
you know Selina is away.'

'Oh yes—I know where Selina is!' And Lionel
Berrington looked round, smiling at every one present,
including Scratch and Parson. He stopped while he
continued to smile and Laura wondered what he
was so much pleased at. She preferred not to ask
—she was sure it was something that wouldn't give
her pleasure; but after waiting a moment her
brother-in-law went on: 'Selina's in Paris, my dear;
that's where Selina is!'

'In Paris?' Laura repeated.

'Yes, in Paris, my dear—God bless her! Where
else do you suppose? Geordie my boy, where
should *you* think your mummy would naturally be?'

'Oh, I don't know,' said Geordie, who had no
reply ready that would express affectingly the desolation of the nursery. 'If I were mummy I'd travel.'

'Well now that's your mummy's idea—she has
gone to travel,' returned the father. 'Were you ever
in Paris, Miss Steet?'

Miss Steet gave a nervous laugh and said No,
but she had been to Boulogne; while to her added
confusion Ferdy announced that he knew where
Paris was—it was in America. 'No, it ain't—it's in
Scotland!' cried Geordie; and Laura asked Lionel
how he knew—whether his wife had written to him.

'Written to me? when did she ever write to me?

No, I saw a fellow in town this morning who saw
her there—at breakfast yesterday.   He came over
last night.   That's how I know my wife's in Paris.
You can't have better proof than that!'

'I suppose it's a very pleasant season there,' the
governess murmured, as if from a sense of duty, in a
distant, discomfortable tone.

'I daresay it's very pleasant indeed—I daresay
it's awfully amusing!' laughed Mr. Berrington.
'Shouldn't you like to run over with me for a few
days, Laura—just to have a go at the theatres?
I don't see why we should always be moping at
home.   We'll take Miss Steet and the children and
give mummy a pleasant surprise.   Now who do you
suppose she was with, in Paris—who do you suppose she was seen with?'

Laura had turned pale, she looked at him hard,
imploringly, in the eyes : there was a name she was
terribly afraid he would mention.   'Oh sir, in that
case we had better go and get ready!' Miss Steet
quavered, betwixt a laugh and a groan, in a spasm
of discretion ; and before Laura knew it she had
gathered Geordie and Ferdy together and swept
them out of the room.   The door closed behind her
with a very quick softness and Lionel remained a
moment staring at it.

'I say, what does she mean?—ain't that damned
impertinent?' he stammered.   'What did she think
I was going to say?   Does she suppose I would say
any harm before—before *her*?   Dash it, does she
suppose I would give away my wife to the servants?'
Then he added, 'And I wouldn't say any harm
before you, Laura.   You are too good and too nice
and I like you too much!'

'Won't you come downstairs? won't you have some tea?' the girl asked, uneasily.

'No, no, I want to stay here—I like this place,' he replied, very gently and reasoningly. 'It's a deuced nice place—it's an awfully jolly room. It used to be this way—always—when I was a little chap. I was a rough one, my dear; I wasn't a pretty little lamb like that pair. I think it's because you look after them—that's what makes 'em so sweet. The one in my time—what was her name? I think it was Bald or Bold—I rather think she found me a handful. I used to kick her shins—I was decidedly vicious. And do *you* see it's kept so well, Laura?' he went on, looking round him. ''Pon my soul, it's the prettiest room in the house. What does she want to go to Paris for when she has got such a charming house? Now can you answer me that, Laura?'

'I suppose she has gone to get some clothes: her dressmaker lives in Paris, you know.'

'Dressmaker? Clothes? Why, she has got whole rooms full of them. Hasn't she got whole rooms full of them?'

'Speaking of clothes I must go and change mine,' said Laura. 'I have been out in the rain—I have been to Plash—I'm decidedly damp.'

'Oh, you have been to Plash? You have seen my mother? I hope she's in very good health.' But before the girl could reply to this he went on: 'Now, I want you to guess who she's in Paris with. Motcomb saw them together—at that place, what's his name? close to the Madeleine.' And as Laura was silent, not wishing at all to guess, he continued —'It's the ruin of any woman, you know; I can't

think what she has got in her head.' Still Laura
said nothing, and as he had hold of her arm, she
having turned away, she led him this time out of
the room. She had a horror of the name, the name
that was in her mind and that was apparently on his
lips, though his tone was so singular, so contempla-
tive. 'My dear girl, she's with Lady Ringrose—
what do you say to that?' he exclaimed, as they
passed along the corridor to the staircase.

'With Lady Ringrose?'

'They went over on Tuesday—they are knocking
about there alone.'

'I don't know Lady Ringrose,' Laura said,
infinitely relieved that the name was not the one
she had feared. Lionel leaned on her arm as they
went downstairs.

'I rather hope not—I promise you she has never
put her foot in this house! If Selina expects to
bring her here I should like half an hour's notice;
yes, half an hour would do. She might as well be
seen with——' And Lionel Berrington checked
himself. 'She has had at least fifty——' And
again he stopped short. 'You must pull me up, you
know, if I say anything you don't like!'

'I don't understand you—let me alone, please!'
the girl broke out, disengaging herself with an
effort from his arm. She hurried down the rest of
the steps and left him there looking after her, and
as she went she heard him give an irrelevant laugh.

IV

SHE determined not to go to dinner—she wished
for that day not to meet him again. He would
drink more—he would be worse—she didn't know
what he might say. Besides she was too angry—
not with him but with Selina—and in addition to
being angry she was sick. She knew who Lady
Ringrose was; she knew so many things to-day
that when she was younger—and only a little—she
had not expected ever to know. Her eyes had been
opened very wide in England and certainly they had
been opened to Lady Ringrose. She had heard
what she had done and perhaps a good deal more,
and it was not very different from what she had
heard of other women. She knew Selina had been to
her house; she had an impression that her ladyship
had been to Selina's, in London, though she herself
had not seen her there. But she had not known
they were so intimate as that—that Selina would rush
over to Paris with her. What they had gone to Paris
for was not necessarily criminal; there were a hundred
reasons, familiar to ladies who were fond of change, of
movement, of the theatres and of new bonnets; but
nevertheless it was the fact of this little excursion quite
as much as the companion that excited Laura's disgust.

She was not ready to say that the companion
was any worse, though Lionel appeared to think so,
than twenty other women who were her sister's
intimates and whom she herself had seen in London,
in Grosvenor Place, and even under the motherly old
beeches at Mellows. But she thought it unpleasant
and base in Selina to go abroad that way, like
a commercial traveller, capriciously, clandestinely,
without giving notice, when she had left her to
understand that she was simply spending three or
four days in town. It was bad taste and bad form,
it was *cabotin* and had the mark of Selina's complete,
irremediable frivolity—the worst accusation (Laura
tried to cling to that opinion) that she laid herself
open to. Of course frivolity that was never ashamed
of itself was like a neglected cold—you could die of
it morally as well as of anything else. Laura knew
this and it was why she was inexpressibly vexed
with her sister. She hoped she should get a letter
from Selina the next morning (Mrs. Berrington would
show at least that remnant of propriety) which would
give her a chance to despatch her an answer that
was already writing itself in her brain. It scarcely
diminished Laura's eagerness for such an opportunity
that she had a vision of Selina's showing her letter,
laughing, across the table, at the place near the
Madeleine, to Lady Ringrose (who would be painted
—Selina herself, to do her justice, was not yet) while
the French waiters, in white aprons, contemplated
ces dames. It was new work for our young lady to
judge of these shades—the gradations, the prob-
abilities of license, and of the side of the line on
which, or rather how far on the wrong side, Lady
Ringrose was situated.

A quarter of an hour before dinner Lionel sent word to her room that she was to sit down without him—he had a headache and wouldn't appear. This was an unexpected grace and it simplified the position for Laura ; so that, smoothing her ruffles, she betook herself to the table. Before doing this however she went back to the schoolroom and told Miss Steet she must contribute her company. She took the governess (the little boys were in bed) downstairs with her and made her sit opposite, thinking she would be a safeguard if Lionel were to change his mind. Miss Steet was more frightened than herself—she was a very shrinking bulwark. The dinner was dull and the conversation rare ; the governess ate three olives and looked at the figures on the spoons. Laura had more than ever her sense of impending calamity ; a draught of misfortune seemed to blow through the house ; it chilled her feet under her chair. The letter she had in her head went out like a flame in the wind and her only thought now was to telegraph to Selina the first thing in the morning, in quite different words. She scarcely spoke to Miss Steet and there was very little the governess could say to her : she had already related her history so often. After dinner she carried her companion into the drawing-room, by the arm, and they sat down to the piano together. They played duets for an hour, mechanically, violently ; Laura had no idea what the music was— she only knew that their playing was execrable. In spite of this—'That's a very nice thing, that last,' she heard a vague voice say, behind her, at the end ; and she became aware that her brother-in-law had joined them again.

Miss Steet was pusillanimous—she retreated on the spot, though Lionel had already forgotten that he was angry at the scandalous way she had carried off the children from the schoolroom. Laura would have gone too if Lionel had not told her that he had something very particular to say to her. That made her want to go more, but she had to listen to him when he expressed the hope that she hadn't taken offence at anything he had said before. He didn't strike her as tipsy now; he had slept it off or got rid of it and she saw no traces of his headache. He was still conspicuously cheerful, as if he had got some good news and were very much encouraged. She knew the news he had got and she might have thought, in view of his manner, that it could not really have seemed to him so bad as he had pretended to think it. It was not the first time however that she had seen him pleased that he had a case against his wife, and she was to learn on this occasion how extreme a satisfaction he could take in his wrongs. She would not sit down again ; she only lingered by the fire, pretending to warm her feet, and he walked to and fro in the long room, where the lamplight to-night was limited, stepping on certain figures of the carpet as if his triumph were alloyed with hesitation.

'I never know how to talk to you—you are so beastly clever,' he said. 'I can't treat you like a little girl in a pinafore—and yet of course you are only a young lady. You're so deuced good—that makes it worse,' he went on, stopping in front of her with his hands in his pockets and the air he himself had of being a good-natured but dissipated boy; with his small stature, his smooth, fat, suffused

face, his round, watery, light-coloured eyes and his
hair growing in curious infantile rings. He had lost
one of his front teeth and always wore a stiff white
scarf, with a pin representing some symbol of the
turf or the chase. 'I don't see why *she* couldn't
have been a little more like you. If I could have
had a shot at you first!'

'I don't care for any compliments at my sister's
expense,' Laura said, with some majesty.

'Oh I say, Laura, don't put on so many frills, as
Selina says. You know what your sister is as well
as I do!' They stood looking at each other a
moment and he appeared to see something in her
face which led him to add—'You know, at any
rate, how little we hit it off.'

'I know you don't love each other—it's too
dreadful.'

'Love each other? she hates me as she'd hate a
hump on her back. She'd do me any devilish turn
she could. There isn't a feeling of loathing that
she doesn't have for me! She'd like to stamp on
me and hear me crack, like a black beetle, and she
never opens her mouth but she insults me.' Lionel
Berrington delivered himself of these assertions
without violence, without passion or the sting of a
new discovery ; there was a familiar gaiety in his
trivial little tone and he had the air of being
so sure of what he said that he did not need to
exaggerate in order to prove enough.

'Oh, Lionel!' the girl murmured, turning pale.
'Is that the particular thing you wished to say to
me ?'

'And you can't say it's my fault—you won't
pretend to do that, will you ?' he went on. 'Ain't

I quiet, ain't I kind, don't I go steady? Haven't I given her every blessed thing she has ever asked for?'

'You haven't given her an example!' Laura replied, with spirit. 'You don't care for anything in the wide world but to amuse yourself, from the beginning of the year to the end. No more does she—and perhaps it's even worse in a woman. You are both as selfish as you can live, with nothing in your head or your heart but your vulgar pleasure, incapable of a concession, incapable of a sacrifice!' She at least spoke with passion; something that had been pent up in her soul broke out and it gave her relief, almost a momentary joy.

It made Lionel Berrington stare; he coloured, but after a moment he threw back his head with laughter. 'Don't you call me kind when I stand here and take all that? If I'm so keen for my pleasure what pleasure do *you* give me? Look at the way I take it, Laura. You ought to do me justice. Haven't I sacrificed my home? and what more can a man do?'

'I don't think you care any more for your home than Selina does. And it's so sacred and so beautiful, God forgive you! You are all blind and senseless and heartless and I don't know what poison is in your veins. There is a curse on you and there will be a judgment!' the girl went on, glowing like a young prophetess.

'What do you want me to do? Do you want me to stay at home and read the Bible?' her companion demanded with an effect of profanity, confronted with her deep seriousness.

'It wouldn't do you any harm, once in a while.'

'There will be a judgment on *her*—that's very

sure, and I know where it will be delivered,' said
Lionel Berrington, indulging in a visible approach
to a wink. 'Have I done the half to her she has
done to me? I won't say the half but the hun-
dredth part? Answer me truly, my dear!'

'I don't know what she has done to you,' said
Laura, impatiently.

'That's exactly what I want to tell you. But
it's difficult. I'll bet you five pounds she's doing it
now!'

'You are too unable to make yourself respected,'
the girl remarked, not shrinking now from the en-
joyment of an advantage—that of feeling herself
superior and taking her opportunity.

Her brother - in - law seemed to feel for the
moment the prick of this observation. 'What has
such a piece of nasty boldness as that to do with
respect? She's the first that ever defied me!' exclaimed the young man, whose aspect somehow
scarcely confirmed this pretension. 'You know all
about her—don't make believe you don't,' he continued in another tone. 'You see everything—
you're one of the sharp ones. There's no use beat-
ing about the bush, Laura—you've lived in this
precious house and you're not so green as that
comes to. Besides, you're so good yourself that
you needn't give a shriek if one is obliged to
say what one means. Why didn't you grow up a
little sooner? Then, over there in New York, it
would certainly have been you I would have made
up to. *You* would have respected me—eh? now
don't say you wouldn't.' He rambled on, turning
about the room again, partly like a person whose
sequences were naturally slow but also a little as if,

though he knew what he had in mind, there were still
a scruple attached to it that he was trying to rub off.

'I take it that isn't what I must sit up to listen
to, Lionel, is it?' Laura said, wearily.

'Why, you don't want to go to bed at nine
o'clock, do you? That's all rot, of course. But I
want you to help me.'

'To help you—how?'

'I'll tell you—but you must give me my head.
I don't know what I said to you before dinner—I
had had too many brandy and sodas. Perhaps I
was too free ; if I was I beg your pardon. I made
the governess bolt—very proper in the superintend-
ent of one's children. Do you suppose they saw
anything? I shouldn't care for that. I did take
half a dozen or so ; I was thirsty and I was awfully
gratified.'

'You have little enough to gratify you.'

'Now that's just where you are wrong. I don't
know when I've fancied anything so much as what
I told you.'

'What you told me?'

'About her being in Paris. I hope she'll stay a
month!'

'I don't understand you,' Laura said.

'Are you very sure, Laura? My dear, it suits
my book! Now you know yourself he's not the
first.'

Laura was silent ; his round eyes were fixed on
her face and she saw something she had not seen
before—a little shining point which on Lionel's
part might represent an idea, but which made his
expression conscious as well as eager. 'He?' she
presently asked. 'Whom are you speaking of?'

'Why, of Charley Crispin, G——' And Lionel Berrington accompanied this name with a startling imprecation.

'What has he to do——?'

'He has everything to do. Isn't he with her there?'

'How should I know? You said Lady Ringrose.'

'Lady Ringrose is a mere blind—and a devilish poor one at that. I'm sorry to have to say it to you, but he's her lover. I mean Selina's. And he ain't the first.'

There was another short silence while they stood opposed, and then Laura asked—and the question was unexpected—'Why do you call him Charley?'

'Doesn't he call me Lion, like all the rest?' said her brother-in-law, staring.

'You're the most extraordinary people. I suppose you have a certain amount of proof before you say such things to me?'

'Proof, I've oceans of proof! And not only about Crispin, but about Deepmere.'

'And pray who is Deepmere?'

'Did you never hear of Lord Deepmere? He has gone to India. That was before you came. I don't say all this for my pleasure, Laura,' Mr. Berrington added.

'Don't you, indeed?' asked the girl with a singular laugh. 'I thought you were so glad.'

'I'm glad to know it but I'm not glad to tell it. When I say I'm glad to know it I mean I'm glad to be fixed at last. Oh, I've got the tip! It's all open country now and I know just how to go. I've gone into it most extensively; there's nothing you can't find out to-day—if you go to the right place. I've—I've——' He hesitated a moment, then went on : 'Well, it's no matter what I've done. I know where I am and it's a great comfort. She's up a tree, if ever a woman was. Now we'll see who's a beetle and who's a toad !' Lionel Berrington concluded, gaily, with some incongruity of metaphor.

'It's not true—it's not true—it's not true,' Laura said, slowly.

'That's just what she'll say—though that's not the way she'll say it. Oh, if she could get off by your saying it for her !—for you, my dear, would be believed.'

'Get off—what do you mean?' the girl demanded, with a coldness she failed to feel, for she was tingling all over with shame and rage.

'Why, what do you suppose I'm talking about? I'm going to haul her up and to have it out.'

'You're going to make a scandal?'

'*Make* it? Bless my soul, it isn't me! And I should think it was made enough. I'm going to appeal to the laws of my country—that's what I'm going to do. She pretends I'm stopped, whatever she does. But that's all gammon—I ain't !'

'I understand—but you won't do anything so horrible,' said Laura, very gently.

'Horrible as you please, but less so than going on in this way; I haven't told you the fiftieth part— you will easily understand that I can't. They are not nice things to say to a girl like you—especially about Deepmere, if you didn't know it. But when they happen you've got to look at them, haven't you? That's the way I look at it.'

'It's not true—it's not true—it's not true,' Laura Wing repeated, in the same way, slowly shaking her head.

'Of course you stand up for your sister—but that's just what I wanted to say to you, that you ought to have some pity for *me* and some sense of justice.   Haven't I always been nice to you? Have you ever had so much as a nasty word from me?'

This appeal touched the girl; she had eaten her brother-in-law's bread for months, she had had the use of all the luxuries with which he was surrounded, and to herself personally she had never known him anything but good-natured.   She made no direct response however; she only said—'Be quiet, be quiet and leave her to me.   I will answer for her.'

'Answer for her—what do you mean?'

'She shall be better—she shall be reasonable— there shall be no more talk of these horrors.   Leave her to me—let me go away with her somewhere.'

'Go away with her?   I wouldn't let you come within a mile of her, if you were *my* sister!'

'Oh, shame, shame!' cried Laura Wing, turning away from him.

She hurried to the door of the room, but he stopped her before she reached it.   He got his back to it, he barred her way and she had to stand there and hear him.   'I haven't said what I wanted—for I told you that I wanted you to help me.   I ain't cruel —I ain't insulting—you can't make out that against me; I'm sure you know in your heart that I've swallowed what would sicken most men.   Therefore I will say that you ought to be fair.   You're too clever not to be; *you* can't pretend to swallow——'

He paused a moment and went on, and she saw it was his idea—an idea very simple and bold. He wanted her to side with him—to watch for him—to help him to get his divorce. He forbore to say that she owed him as much for the hospitality and protection she had in her poverty enjoyed, but she was sure that was in his heart. 'Of course she's your sister, but when one's sister's a perfect bad 'un there's no law to force one to jump into the mud to save her. It *is* mud, my dear, and mud up to your neck. You had much better think of her children—you had much better stop in *my* boat.'

'Do you ask me to help you with evidence against her?' the girl murmured. She had stood there passive, waiting while he talked, covering her face with her hands, which she parted a little, looking at him.

He hesitated a moment. 'I ask you not to deny what you have seen—what you feel to be true.'

'Then of the abominations of which you say you have proof, you haven't proof.'

'Why haven't I proof?'

'If you want *me* to come forward!'

'I shall go into court with a strong case. You may do what you like. But I give you notice and I expect you not to forget that I have given it. Don't forget—because you'll be asked—that I have told you to-night where she is and with whom she is and what measures I intend to take.'

'Be asked—be asked?' the girl repeated.

'Why, of course you'll be cross-examined.'

'Oh, mother, mother!' cried Laura Wing. Her hands were over her face again and as Lionel Berrington, opening the door, let her pass, she burst into tears.   He looked after her, distressed, compunctious, half-ashamed, and he exclaimed to himself—'The bloody brute, the bloody brute!'   But the words had reference to his wife.

V

'AND are you telling me the perfect truth when you say that Captain Crispin was not there?'

'The perfect truth?' Mrs. Berrington straightened herself to her height, threw back her head and measured her interlocutress up and down; it is to be surmised that this was one of the many ways in which she knew she looked very handsome indeed. Her interlocutress was her sister, and even in a discussion with a person long since initiated she was not incapable of feeling that her beauty was a new advantage. On this occasion she had at first the air of depending upon it mainly to produce an effect upon Laura; then, after an instant's reflection, she determined to arrive at her result in another way. She exchanged her expression of scorn (of resentment at her veracity's being impugned) for a look of gentle amusement; she smiled patiently, as if she remembered that of course Laura couldn't understand of what an impertinence she had been guilty. There was a quickness of perception and lightness of hand which, to her sense, her American sister had never acquired: the girl's earnest, almost barbarous probity blinded her to the importance of certain pleasant little forms. 'My poor child, the things you do say!

One doesn't put a question about the perfect truth in
a manner that implies that a person is telling a
perfect lie.   However, as it's only you, I don't mind
satisfying your clumsy curiosity.   I haven't the least
idea whether Captain Crispin was there or not.   I
know nothing of his movements and he doesn't keep
me informed—why should he, poor man?—of his
whereabouts.   He was not there for me—isn't that
all that need interest you?   As far as I was concerned he might have been at the North Pole.   I
neither saw him nor heard of him.   I didn't see the
end of his nose!' Selina continued, still with her
wiser, tolerant brightness, looking straight into her
sister's eyes.   Her own were clear and lovely and
she was but little less handsome than if she had been
proud and freezing.   Laura wondered at her more
and more ; stupefied suspense was now almost the
girl's constant state of mind.

Mrs. Berrington had come back from Paris the
day before but had not proceeded to Mellows the
same night, though there was more than one train
she might have taken.   Neither had she gone to the
house in Grosvenor Place but had spent the night at
an hotel.   Her husband was absent again ; he was
supposed to be in Grosvenor Place, so that they had
not yet met.   Little as she was a woman to admit
that she had been in the wrong she was known to
have granted later that at this moment she had made
a mistake in not going straight to her own house.
It had given Lionel a degree of advantage, made it
appear perhaps a little that she had a bad conscience
and was afraid to face him.   But she had had her
reasons for putting up at an hotel, and she thought
it unnecessary to express them very definitely.   She

came home by a morning train, the second day, and
arrived before luncheon, of which meal she partook
in the company of her sister and in that of Miss
Steet and the children, sent for in honour of the
occasion. After luncheon she let the governess go
but kept Scratch and Parson—kept them on ever so
long in the morning-room where she remained; longer
than she had ever kept them before. Laura was
conscious that she ought to have been pleased at
this, but there was a perversity even in Selina's
manner of doing right; for she wished immensely
now to see her alone—she had something so serious
to say to her. Selina hugged her children repeatedly,
encouraging their sallies; she laughed extravagantly
at the artlessness of their remarks, so that at table
Miss Steet was quite abashed by her unusual high
spirits. Laura was unable to question her about
Captain Crispin and Lady Ringrose while Geordie
and Ferdy were there: they would not understand,
of course, but names were always reflected in their
limpid little minds and they gave forth the image
later—often in the most extraordinary connections.
It was as if Selina knew what she was waiting for
and were determined to make her wait. The girl
wished her to go to her room, that she might follow
her there. But Selina showed no disposition to
retire, and one could never entertain the idea for her,
on any occasion, that it would be suitable that she
should change her dress. The dress she wore—
whatever it was—was too becoming to her, and
to the moment, for that. Laura noticed how the
very folds of her garment told that she had been to
Paris; she had spent only a week there but the
mark of her *couturière* was all over her: it was simply

to confer with this great artist that, from her own
account, she had crossed the Channel. The signs of
the conference were so conspicuous that it was as if
she had said, 'Don't you see the proof that it was
for nothing but *chiffons?*' She walked up and down
the room with Geordie in her arms, in an access of
maternal tenderness; he was much too big to nestle
gracefully in her bosom, but that only made her
seem younger, more flexible, fairer in her tall, strong
slimness. Her distinguished figure bent itself hither
and thither, but always in perfect freedom, as she
romped with her children; and there was another
moment, when she came slowly down the room,
holding one of them in each hand and singing to
them while they looked up at her beauty, charmed
and listening and a little surprised at such new ways
—a moment when she might have passed for some
grave, antique statue of a young matron, or even for
a picture of Saint Cecilia. This morning, more than
ever, Laura was struck with her air of youth, the
inextinguishable freshness that would have made
any one exclaim at her being the mother of such
bouncing little boys. Laura had always admired
her, thought her the prettiest woman in London, the
beauty with the finest points; and now these points
were so vivid (especially her finished slenderness and
the grace, the natural elegance of every turn—the
fall of her shoulders had never looked so perfect)
that the girl almost detested them: they appeared
to her a kind of advertisement of danger and even of
shame.

Miss Steet at last came back for the children,
and as soon as she had taken them away Selina
observed that she would go over to Plash—just as

she was : she rang for her hat and jacket and for the carriage. Laura could see that she would not give her just yet the advantage of a retreat to her room. The hat and jacket were quickly brought, but after they were put on Selina kept her maid in the drawing-room, talking to her a long time, telling her elaborately what she wished done with the things she had brought from Paris. Before the maid departed the carriage was announced, and the servant, leaving the door of the room open, hovered within earshot. Laura then, losing patience, turned out the maid and closed the door ; she stood before her sister, who was prepared for her drive. Then she asked her abruptly, fiercely, but colouring with her question, whether Captain Crispin had been in Paris. We have heard Mrs. Berrington's answer, with which her strenuous sister was imperfectly satisfied ; a fact the perception of which it doubtless was that led Selina to break out, with a greater show of indignation : 'I never heard of such extraordinary ideas for a girl to have, and such extraordinary things for a girl to talk about ! My dear, you have acquired a freedom—you have emancipated yourself from conventionality—and I suppose I must congratulate you.' Laura only stood there, with her eyes fixed, without answering the sally, and Selina went on, with another change of tone : 'And pray if he *was* there, what is there so monstrous ? Hasn't it happened that he is in London when I am there ? Why is it then so awful that he should be in Paris ?'

'Awful, awful, too awful,' murmured Laura, with intense gravity, still looking at her—looking all the more fixedly that she knew how little Selina liked it.

'My dear, you do indulge in a style of innuendo, for a respectable young woman!' Mrs. Berrington exclaimed, with an angry laugh. 'You have ideas that when I was a girl——' She paused, and her sister saw that she had not the assurance to finish her sentence on that particular note.

'Don't talk about my innuendoes and my ideas— you might remember those in which I have heard you indulge! Ideas? what ideas did I ever have before I came here?' Laura Wing asked, with a trembling voice. 'Don't pretend to be shocked, Selina; that's too cheap a defence. You have said things to me—if you choose to talk of freedom! What is the talk of your house and what does one hear if one lives with you? I don't care what I hear now (it's all odious and there's little choice and my sweet sensibility has gone God knows where!) and I'm very glad if you understand that I don't care what I say. If one talks about your affairs, my dear, one mustn't be too particular!' the girl continued, with a flash of passion.

Mrs. Berrington buried her face in her hands. 'Merciful powers, to be insulted, to be covered with outrage, by one's wretched little sister!' she moaned.

'I think you should be thankful there is one human being—however wretched—who cares enough for you to care about the truth in what concerns you,' Laura said. 'Selina, Selina—are you hideously deceiving us?'

'Us?' Selina repeated, with a singular laugh. 'Whom do you mean by us?'

Laura Wing hesitated; she had asked herself whether it would be best she should let her sister

know the dreadful scene she had had with Lionel;
but she had not, in her mind, settled that point.
However, it was settled now in an instant. 'I don't
mean your friends—those of them that I have seen.
I don't think *they* care a straw—I have never seen
such people. But last week Lionel spoke to me—he
told me he *knew* it, as a certainty.'

'Lionel spoke to you?' said Mrs. Berrington,
holding up her head with a stare. 'And what is it
that he knows?'

'That Captain Crispin was in Paris and that you
were with him. He believes you went there to meet
him.'

'He said this to *you*?'

'Yes, and much more—I don't know why I
should make a secret of it.'

'The disgusting beast!' Selina exclaimed slowly,
solemnly. 'He enjoys the right—the legal right—to
pour forth his vileness upon *me;* but when he is so
lost to every feeling as to begin to talk to you in
such a way——!' And Mrs. Berrington paused, in
the extremity of her reprobation.

'Oh, it was not his talk that shocked me—it was
his believing it,' the girl replied. 'That, I confess,
made an impression on me.'

'Did it indeed? I'm infinitely obliged to you!
You are a tender, loving little sister.'

'Yes, I am, if it's tender to have cried about you
—all these days—till I'm blind and sick!' Laura
replied. 'I hope you are prepared to meet him.
His mind is quite made up to apply for a divorce.'

Laura's voice almost failed her as she said this—
it was the first time that in talking with Selina she
had uttered that horrible word. She had heard it

however, often enough on the lips of others; it had
been bandied lightly enough in her presence under
those somewhat austere ceilings of Mellows, of which
the admired decorations and mouldings, in the taste
of the middle of the last century, all in delicate
plaster and reminding her of Wedgewood pottery,
consisted of slim festoons, urns and trophies and
knotted ribbons, so many symbols of domestic affec-
tion and irrevocable union. Selina herself had flashed
it at her with light superiority, as if it were some
precious jewel kept in reserve, which she could con-
vert at any moment into specie, so that it would
constitute a happy provision for her future. The
idea—associated with her own point of view—was
apparently too familiar to Mrs. Berrington to be the
cause of her changing colour; it struck her indeed,
as presented by Laura, in a ludicrous light, for her
pretty eyes expanded a moment and she smiled
pityingly. 'Well, you are a poor dear innocent, after
all. Lionel would be about as able to divorce me—
even if I were the most abandoned of my sex—as he
would be to write a leader in the *Times.*'

'I know nothing about that,' said Laura.

'So I perceive—as I also perceive that you must
have shut your eyes very tight. Should you like to
know a few of the reasons—heaven forbid I should
attempt to go over them all; there are millions!—
why his hands are tied?'

'Not in the least.'

'Should you like to know that his own life is too
base for words and that his impudence in talking
about me would be sickening if it weren't grotesque?'
Selina went on, with increasing emotion. 'Should
you like me to tell you to what he has stooped—to

the very gutter—and the charming history of his
relations with——'

'No, I don't want you to tell me anything of
the sort,' Laura interrupted. 'Especially as you
were just now so pained by the license of my own
allusions.'

'You listen to him then—but it suits your purpose not to listen to me !'

'Oh, Selina, Selina !' the girl almost shrieked,
turning away.

'Where have your eyes been, or your senses, or
your powers of observation ? You can be clever
enough when it suits you !' Mrs. Berrington continued, throwing off another ripple of derision. 'And
now perhaps, as the carriage is waiting, you will let
me go about my duties.'

Laura turned again and stopped her, holding her
arm as she passed toward the door. 'Will you
swear—will you swear by everything that is most
sacred ?'

'Will I swear what ?' And now she thought
Selina visibly blanched.

'That you didn't lay eyes on Captain Crispin in
Paris.'

Mrs. Berrington hesitated, but only for an instant.
'You are really too odious, but as you are pinching
me to death I will swear, to get away from you. I
never laid eyes on him.'

The organs of vision which Mrs. Berrington was
ready solemnly to declare that she had not mis-
applied were, as her sister looked into them, an
abyss of indefinite prettiness. The girl had sounded
them before without discovering a conscience at the
bottom of them, and they had never helped any one

to find out anything about their possessor except
that she was one of the beauties of London.   Even
while Selina spoke Laura had a cold, horrible sense
of not believing her, and at the same time a desire,
colder still, to extract a reiteration of the pledge.
Was it the asseveration of her innocence that she
wished her to repeat, or only the attestation of her
falsity ?   One way or the other it seemed to her
that this would settle something, and she went on
inexorably—'By our dear mother's memory—by
our poor father's ? '

'By my mother's, by my father's,' said Mrs
Berrington, 'and by that of any other member of
the family you like!' Laura let her go ; she had
not been pinching her, as Selina described the
pressure, but had clung to her with insistent hands.
As she opened the door Selina said, in a changed
voice : 'I suppose it's no use to ask you if you care
to drive to Plash.'

'No, thank you, I don't care—I shall take a
walk.'

'I suppose, from that, that your friend Lady
Davenant has gone.'

'No, I think she is still there.'

'That's a bore!' Selina exclaimed, as she went
off.

VI

Laura Wing hastened to her room to prepare herself for her walk; but when she reached it she simply fell on her knees, shuddering, beside her bed. She buried her face in the soft counterpane of wadded silk; she remained there a long time, with a kind of aversion to lifting it again to the day. It burned with horror and there was coolness in the smooth glaze of the silk. It seemed to her that she had been concerned in a hideous transaction, and her uppermost feeling was, strangely enough, that she was ashamed—not of her sister but of herself. She did not believe her—that was at the bottom of everything, and she had made her lie, she had brought out her perjury, she had associated it with the sacred images of the dead. She took no walk, she remained in her room, and quite late, towards six o'clock, she heard on the gravel, outside of her windows, the wheels of the carriage bringing back Mrs. Berrington. She had evidently been elsewhere as well as to Plash; no doubt she had been to the vicarage—she was capable even of that. She could pay 'duty-visits,' like that (she called at the vicarage about three times a year), and she could go and be nice to her mother-in-law with her fresh lips still fresher for the lie she had just told. For it was as definite as an aching nerve to Laura that she did not believe her, and if she did not believe her the words she had spoken were a lie. It was the lie, the lie to *her* and which she had dragged out of her that seemed to the girl the ugliest thing. If she had admitted her folly, if she had explained, attenuated, sophisticated, there would have been a difference in her favour ; but now she was bad because she was hard. She had a surface of polished metal. And she could make plans and calculate, she could act and do things for a particular effect. She could go straight to old Mrs. Berrington and to the parson's wife and his many daughters (just as she had kept the children after luncheon, on purpose, so long) because that looked innocent and domestic and denoted a mind without a feather's weight upon it.

A servant came to the young lady's door to tell her that tea was ready; and on her asking who else was below (for she had heard the wheels of a second vehicle just after Selina's return), she learned that Lionel had come back. At this news she requested that some tea should be brought to her room—she determined not to go to dinner. When the dinner-hour came she sent down word that she had a head-ache, that she was going to bed. She wondered whether Selina would come to her (she could forget disagreeable scenes amazingly) ; but her fervent hope that she would stay away was gratified. Indeed she would have another call upon her attention if her meeting with her husband was half as much of a concussion as was to have been expected. Laura had found herself listening hard, after knowing that

her brother-in-law was in the house : she half expected to hear indications of violence—loud cries or
the sound of a scuffle.   It was a matter of course to
her that some dreadful scene had not been slow to
take place, something that discretion should keep her
out of even if she had not been too sick.   She did
not go to bed—partly because she didn't know what
might happen in the house.   But she was restless
also for herself : things had reached a point when it
seemed to her that she must make up her mind.
She left her candles unlighted—she sat up till the
small hours, in the glow of the fire.   What had
been settled by her scene with Selina was that worse
things were to come (looking into her fire, as the
night went on, she had a rare prevision of the
catastrophe that hung over the house), and she considered, or tried to consider, what it would be best
for her, in anticipation, to do.   The first thing was
to take flight.

It may be related without delay that Laura Wing
did not take flight and that though the circumstance
detracts from the interest that should be felt in her
character she did not even make up her mind.   That
was not so easy when action had to ensue.   At the
same time she had not the excuse of a conviction
that by not acting—that is by not withdrawing from
her brother-in-law's roof—she should be able to hold
Selina up to her duty, to drag her back into the
straight path.   The hopes connected with that pro-
ject were now a phase that she had left behind her ;
she had not to-day an illusion about her sister large
enough to cover a sixpence.   She had passed through
the period of superstition, which had lasted the longest
—the time when it seemed to her, as at first, a kind

of profanity to doubt of Selina and judge her, the elder sister whose beauty and success she had ever been proud of and who carried herself, though with the most good-natured fraternisings, as one native to an upper air. She had called herself in moments of early penitence for irrepressible suspicion a little presumptuous prig : so strange did it seem to her at first, the impulse of criticism in regard to her bright protectress. But the revolution was over and she had a desolate, lonely freedom which struck her as not the most cynical thing in the world only because Selina's behaviour was more so. She supposed she should learn, though she was afraid of the know-ledge, what had passed between that lady and her husband while her vigil ached itself away. But it appeared to her the next day, to her surprise, that nothing was changed in the situation save that Selina knew at present how much more she was suspected. As this had not a chastening effect upon Mrs. Berrington nothing had been gained by Laura's appeal to her. Whatever Lionel had said to his wife he said nothing to Laura : he left her at perfect liberty to forget the subject he had opened up to her so luminously. This was very characteristic of his good-nature ; it had come over him that after all she wouldn't like it, and if the free use of the gray ponies could make up to her for the shock she might order them every day in the week and banish the unpleasant episode from her mind.

Laura ordered the gray ponies very often : she drove herself all over the country. She visited not only the neighbouring but the distant poor, and she never went out without stopping for one of the vicar's fresh daughters. Mellows was now half the

time full of visitors and when it was not its master
and mistress were staying with their friends either
together or singly. Sometimes (almost always when
she was asked) Laura Wing accompanied her sister
and on two or three occasions she paid an independent visit. Selina had often told her that she wished
her to have her own friends, so that the girl now felt
a great desire to show her that she had them. She
had arrived at no decision whatever ; she had embraced in intention no particular course. She drifted
on, shutting her eyes, averting her head and, as it
seemed to herself, hardening her heart. This ad-
mission will doubtless suggest to the reader that she
was a weak, inconsequent, spasmodic young person,
with a standard not really, or at any rate not con-
tinuously, high ; and I have no desire that she shall
appear anything but what she was. It must even be
related of her that since she could not escape and
live in lodgings and paint fans (there were reasons
why this combination was impossible) she determined to try and be happy in the given circumstances—to float in shallow, turbid water. She gave
up the attempt to understand the cynical *modus
vivendi* at which her companions seemed to have
arrived ; she knew it was not final but it served
them sufficiently for the time ; and if it served them
why should it not serve her, the dependent, impe-
cunious, tolerated little sister, representative of the
class whom it behoved above all to mind their own
business ? The time was coming round when they
would all move up to town, and there, in the crowd,
with the added movement, the strain would be less
and indifference easier.

Whatever Lionel had said to his wife that even-

ing she had found something to say to him : that
Laura could see, though not so much from any
change in the simple expression of his little red face
and in the vain bustle of his existence as from the
grand manner in which Selina now carried herself.
She was 'smarter' than ever and her waist was
smaller and her back straighter and the fall of her
shoulders finer ; her long eyes were more oddly
charming and the extreme detachment of her elbows
from her sides conduced still more to the exhibition
of her beautiful arms.   So she floated, with a serenity
not disturbed by a general tardiness, through the
interminable succession of her engagements.   Her
photographs were not to be purchased in the
Burlington Arcade — she had kept out of that ;
but she looked more than ever as they would have
represented her if they had been obtainable there.
There were times when Laura thought her brother-
in-law's formless desistence too frivolous for nature :
it even gave her a sense of deeper dangers.   It was
as if he had been digging away in the dark and they
would all tumble into the hole.   It happened to her
to ask herself whether the things he had said to her
the afternoon he fell upon her in the schoolroom had
not all been a clumsy practical joke, a crude desire
to scare, that of a schoolboy playing with a sheet in
the dark ; or else brandy and soda, which came to
the same thing.   However this might be she was
obliged to recognise that the impression of brandy
and soda had not again been given her.   More
striking still however was Selina's capacity to recover
from shocks and condone imputations ; she kissed
again—kissed Laura—without tears, and proposed
problems connected with the rearrangement of trim-

mings and of the flowers at dinner, as candidly—as
earnestly—as if there had never been an intenser
question between them. Captain Crispin was not
mentioned ; much less of course, so far as Laura
was concerned, was he seen. But Lady Ringrose
appeared ; she came down for two days, during an
absence of Lionel's. Laura, to her surprise, found
her no such Jezebel but a clever little woman with a
single eye-glass and short hair who had read Lecky
and could give her useful hints about water-colours :
a reconciliation that encouraged the girl, for this was
the direction in which it now seemed to her best
that she herself should grow.

VII

IN Grosvenor Place, on Sunday afternoon, during the
first weeks of the season, Mrs. Berrington was usually
at home : this indeed was the only time when a
visitor who had not made an appointment could hope
to be admitted to her presence.   Very few hours in
the twenty-four did she spend in her own house.
Gentlemen calling on these occasions rarely found
her sister : Mrs. Berrington had the field to herself.
It was understood between the pair that Laura
should take this time for going to see her old
women : it was in that manner that Selina qualified the girl's independent social resources.   The old
women however were not a dozen in number ; they
consisted mainly of Lady Davenant and the elder
Mrs. Berrington, who had a house in Portman Street.
Lady Davenant lived at Queen's Gate and also was
usually at home of a Sunday afternoon : her visitors
were not all men, like Selina Berrington's, and
Laura's maidenly bonnet was not a false note in her
drawing-room.   Selina liked her sister, naturally
enough, to make herself useful, but of late, somehow,
they had grown rarer, the occasions that depended in
any degree upon her aid, and she had never been
much appealed to—though it would have seemed

natural she should be——on behalf of the weekly
chorus of gentlemen.   It came to be recognised on
Selina's part that nature had dedicated her more to
the relief of old women than to that of young men.
Laura had a distinct sense of interfering with the
free interchange of anecdote and pleasantry that
went on at her sister's fireside : the anecdotes were
mostly such an immense secret that they could not
be told fairly if she were there, and she had their
privacy on her conscience.   There was an exception
however ; when Selina expected Americans she
naturally asked her to stay at home : not apparently
so much because their conversation would be good
for her as because hers would be good for them.

One Sunday, about the middle of May, Laura
Wing prepared herself to go and see Lady Davenant, who had made a long absence from town at
Easter but would now have returned.   The weather
was charming, she had from the first established her
right to tread the London streets alone (if she was a
poor girl she could have the detachment as well as
the helplessness of it) and she promised herself the
pleasure of a walk along the park, where the new
grass was bright.   A moment before she quitted the
house her sister sent for her to the drawing-room ;
the servant gave her a note scrawled in pencil :
' That man from New York is here——Mr. Wendover,
who brought me the introduction the other day from
the Schoolings.   He's rather a dose——you must
positively come down and talk to him.   Take him
out with you if you can.'   The description was not
alluring, but Selina had never made a request of her
to which the girl had not instantly responded : it
seemed to her she was there for that.   She joined

the circle in the drawing-room and found that it consisted of five persons, one of whom was Lady Ringrose.   Lady Ringrose was at all times and in all
places a fitful apparition ; she had described herself
to Laura during her visit at Mellows as 'a bird on
the branch.'   She had no fixed habit of receiving on
Sunday, she was in and out as she liked, and she was
one of the few specimens of her sex who, in Grosvenor Place, ever turned up, as she said, on the occasions to which I allude.   Of the three gentlemen
two were known to Laura ; she could have told you
at least that the big one with the red hair was in the
Guards and the other in the Rifles ; the latter looked
like a rosy child and as if he ought to be sent up to
play with Geordie and Ferdy : his social nickname
indeed was the Baby.   Selina's admirers were of all
ages—they ranged from infants to octogenarians.

She introduced the third gentleman to her sister ;
a tall, fair, slender young man who suggested that
he had made a mistake in the shade of his tight,
perpendicular coat, ordering it of too heavenly a blue.
This added however to the candour of his appearance,
and if he was a dose, as Selina had described
him, he could only operate beneficently.   There
were moments when Laura's heart rather yearned
towards her countrymen, and now, though she was
preoccupied and a little disappointed at having been
detained, she tried to like Mr. Wendover, whom her
sister had compared invidiously, as it seemed to her,
with her other companions.   It struck her that his
surface at least was as glossy as theirs.   The Baby,
whom she remembered to have heard spoken of as a
dangerous flirt, was in conversation with Lady Ringrose and the guardsman with Mrs. Berrington ; so

she did her best to entertain the American visitor,
as to whom any one could easily see (she thought)
that he had brought a letter of introduction—he
wished so to maintain the credit of those who had
given it to him.   Laura scarcely knew these people,
American friends of her sister who had spent a
period of festivity in London and gone back across
the sea before her own advent ; but Mr. Wendover
gave her all possible information about them.   He
lingered upon them, returned to them, corrected
statements he had made at first, discoursed upon them
earnestly and exhaustively.   He seemed to fear to
leave them, lest he should find nothing again so
good, and he indulged in a parallel that was almost
elaborate between Miss Fanny and Miss Katie.
Selina told her sister afterwards that she had over-
heard him—that he talked of them as if he had
been a nursemaid ; upon which Laura defended the
young man even to extravagance.   She reminded
her sister that people in London were always saying
Lady Mary and Lady Susan : why then shouldn't
Americans use the Christian name, with the humbler
prefix with which they had to content themselves ?
There had been a time when Mrs. Berrington had
been happy enough to be Miss Lina, even though
she was the elder sister ; and the girl liked to think
there were still old friends—friends of the family,
at home, for whom, even should she live to sixty
years of spinsterhood, she would never be anything but Miss Laura.   This was as good as Donna
Anna or Donna Elvira : English people could never
call people as other people did, for fear of resembling
the servants.

Mr. Wendover was very attentive, as well as

communicative; however his letter might be regarded
in Grosvenor Place he evidently took it very seriously
himself; but his eyes wandered considerably, none
the less, to the other side of the room, and Laura
felt that though he had often seen persons like her
before (not that he betrayed this too crudely) he had
never seen any one like Lady Ringrose. His glance
rested also on Mrs. Berrington, who, to do her
justice, abstained from showing, by the way she
returned it, that she wished her sister to get him out
of the room. Her smile was particularly pretty on
Sunday afternoons and he was welcome to enjoy it
as a part of the decoration of the place. Whether or
no the young man should prove interesting he was at
any rate interested; indeed she afterwards learned
that what Selina deprecated in him was the fact that
he would eventually display a fatiguing intensity of
observation. He would be one of the sort who
noticed all kinds of little things—things she never
saw or heard of—in the newspapers or in society,
and would call upon her (a dreadful prospect) to
explain or even to defend them. She had not come
there to explain England to the Americans; the
more particularly as her life had been a burden to
her during the first years of her marriage through
her having to explain America to the English. As
for defending England to her countrymen she had
much rather defend it *from* them: there were too
many—too many for those who were already there.
This was the class she wished to spare—she didn't
care about the English. They could obtain an eye
for an eye and a cutlet for a cutlet by going over
there; which she had no desire to do—not for all
the cutlets in Christendom!

When Mr. Wendover and Laura had at last cut
loose from the Schoolings he let her know confiden-
tially that he had come over really to see London :
he had time, that year ; he didn't know when he
should have it again (if ever, as he said) and he had
made up his mind that this was about the best use
he could make of four months and a half. He had
heard so much of it ; it was talked of so much to-
day ; a man felt as if he ought to know something
about it. Laura wished the others could hear this
—that England was coming up, was making her way
at last to a place among the topics of societies more
universal. She thought Mr. Wendover after all
remarkably like an Englishman, in spite of his saying that he believed she had resided in London quite
a time. He talked a great deal about things being
characteristic, and wanted to know, lowering his
voice to make the inquiry, whether Lady Ringrose
were not particularly so. He had heard of her very
often, he said ; and he observed that it was very
interesting to see her : he could not have used a
different tone if he had been speaking of the prime
minister or the laureate. Laura was ignorant of
what he had heard of Lady Ringrose ; she doubted
whether it could be the same as what she had heard
from her brother-in-law : if this had been the case
he never would have mentioned it. She foresaw
that his friends in London would have a good deal
to do in the way of telling him whether this or that
were characteristic or not ; he would go about in
much the same way that English travellers did in
America, fixing his attention mainly on society (he
let Laura know that this was especially what he
wished to go into) and neglecting the antiquities and

sights, quite as if he failed to believe in their importance. He would ask questions it was impossible to answer ; as to whether for instance society were very different in the two countries. If you said yes you gave a wrong impression and if you said no you didn't give a right one : that was the kind of thing that Selina had suffered from. Laura found her new acquaintance, on the present occasion and later, more philosophically analytic of his impressions than those of her countrymen she had hitherto encountered in her new home : the latter, in regard to such impressions, usually exhibited either a profane levity or a tendency to mawkish idealism.

Mrs. Berrington called out at last to Laura that she must not stay if she had prepared herself to go out : whereupon the girl, having nodded and smiled good-bye at the other members of the circle, took a more formal leave of Mr. Wendover— expressed the hope, as an American girl does in such a case, that they should see him again. Selina asked him to come and dine three days later ; which was as much as to say that relations might be suspended till then. Mr. Wendover took it so, and having accepted the invitation he departed at the same time as Laura. He passed out of the house with her and in the street she asked him which way he was going. He was too tender, but she liked him ; he appeared not to deal in chaff and that was a change that relieved her—she had so often had to pay out that coin when she felt wretchedly poor. She hoped he would ask her leave to go with her the way she was going—and this not on particular but on general grounds. It would be American, it

would remind her of old times ; she should like him
to be as American as that.   There was no reason
for her taking so quick an interest in his nature,
inasmuch as she had not fallen under his spell ; but
there were moments when she felt a whimsical desire
to be reminded of the way people felt and acted at
home.   Mr. Wendover did not disappoint her, and
the bright chocolate-coloured vista of the Fifth
Avenue seemed to surge before her as he said, ' May
I have the pleasure of making my direction the same
as yours ? ' and moved round, systematically, to take
his place between her and the curbstone.   She had
never walked much with young men in America
(she had been brought up in the new school, the
school of attendant maids and the avoidance of
certain streets) and she had very often done so in
England, in the country ; yet, as at the top of
Grosvenor Place she crossed over to the park, pro-
posing they should take that way, the breath of her
native land was in her nostrils.   It was certainly
only an American who could have the tension of
Mr. Wendover ;   his solemnity almost made her
laugh, just as her eyes grew dull when people
' slanged ' each other hilariously in her sister's house ;
but at the same time he gave her a feeling of high
respectability.   It would be respectable still if she
were to go on with him indefinitely—if she never
were to come home at all.   He asked her after a
while, as they went, whether he had violated the
custom of the English in offering her his company ;
whether in that country a gentleman might walk with
a young lady—the first time he saw her—not because
their roads lay together but for the sake of the walk.

 ' Why should it matter to me whether it is the

custom of the English? I am not English,' said
Laura Wing. Then her companion explained that
he only wanted a general guidance—that with her
(she was so kind) he had not the sense of having
taken a liberty. The point was simply—and rather
comprehensively and strenuously he began to set
forth the point. Laura interrupted him; she said
she didn't care about it and he almost irritated her
by telling her she was kind. She was, but she was
not pleased at its being recognised so soon; and he
was still too importunate when he asked her whether
she continued to go by American usage, didn't find
that if one lived there one had to conform in a great
many ways to the English. She was weary of the
perpetual comparison, for she not only heard it from
others—she heard it a great deal from herself. She
held that there were certain differences you felt, if
you belonged to one or the other nation, and that
was the end of it: there was no use trying to
express them. Those you *could* express were not
real or not important ones and were not worth talking about. Mr. Wendover asked her if she liked
English society and if it were superior to American;
also if the tone were very high in London. She
thought his questions 'academic'—the term she
used to see applied in the *Times* to certain speeches
in Parliament. Bending his long leanness over her
(she had never seen a man whose material presence
was so insubstantial, so unoppressive) and walking
almost sidewise, to give her a proper attention, he
struck her as innocent, as incapable of guessing that
she had had a certain observation of life. They
were talking about totally different things: English
society, as he asked her judgment upon it and she

had happened to see it, was an affair that he didn't
suspect.   If she were to give him that judgment it
would be more than he doubtless bargained for ; but
she would do it not to make him open his eyes—only
to relieve herself.   She had thought of that before
in regard to two or three persons she had met—of
the satisfaction of breaking out with some of her
feelings.   It would make little difference whether
the person understood her or not ; the one who
should do so best would be far from understanding
everything.   ' I want to get out of it, please—out of
the set I live in, the one I have tumbled into
through my sister, the people you saw just now.
There are thousands of people in London who are
different from that and ever so much nicer ; but
I don't see them, I don't know how to get at them ;
and after all, poor dear man, what power have you
to help me ? '   That was in the last analysis the gist
of what she had to say.

Mr. Wendover asked her about Selina in the
tone of a person who thought Mrs. Berrington a
very important phenomenon, and that by itself was
irritating to Laura Wing.   Important—gracious
goodness, no !   She might have to live with her, to
hold her tongue about her ; but at least she was not
bound to exaggerate her significance.   The young
man forbore decorously to make use of the expression, but she could see that he supposed Selina to be
a professional beauty and she guessed that as this
product had not yet been domesticated in the
western world the desire to behold it, after having
read so much about it, had been one of the motives
of Mr. Wendover's pilgrimage.   Mrs. Schooling, who
must have been a goose, had told him that Mrs.

Berrington, though transplanted, was the finest flower of a rich, ripe society and as clever and virtuous as she was beautiful. Meanwhile Laura knew what Selina thought of Fanny Schooling and her incurable provinciality. 'Now was that a good example of London talk—what I heard (I only heard a little of it, but the conversation was more general before you came in) in your sister's drawing-room? I don't mean literary, intellectual talk—I suppose there are special places to hear that; I mean—I mean——' Mr. Wendover went on with a deliberation which gave his companion an opportunity to interrupt him. They had arrived at Lady Davenant's door and she cut his meaning short. A fancy had taken her, on the spot, and the fact that it was whimsical seemed only to recommend it.

'If you want to hear London talk there will be some very good going on in here,' she said. 'If you would like to come in with me——?'

'Oh, you are very kind—I should be delighted,' replied Mr. Wendover, endeavouring to emulate her own more rapid processes. They stepped into the porch and the young man, anticipating his companion, lifted the knocker and gave a postman's rap. She laughed at him for this and he looked bewildered; the idea of taking him in with her had become agreeably exhilarating. Their acquaintance, in that moment, took a long jump. She explained to him who Lady Davenant was and that if he was in search of the characteristic it would be a pity he shouldn't know her; and then she added, before he could put the question:

'And what I am doing is *not* in the least usual. No, it is not the custom for young ladies here to take strange gentlemen off to call on their friends the first time they see them.'

'So that Lady Davenant will think it rather extraordinary?' Mr. Wendover eagerly inquired; not as if that idea frightened him, but so that his observation on this point should also be well founded. He had entered into Laura's proposal with complete serenity.

'Oh, most extraordinary!' said Laura, as they went in. The old lady however concealed such surprise as she may have felt, and greeted Mr. Wendover as if he were any one of fifty familiars. She took him altogether for granted and asked him no questions about his arrival, his departure, his hotel or his business in England. He noticed, as he afterwards confided to Laura, her omission of these forms; but he was not wounded by it—he only made a mark against it as an illustration of the difference between English and American manners: in New York people always asked the arriving stranger the first thing about the steamer and the hotel. Mr. Wendover appeared greatly impressed with Lady Davenant's antiquity, though he confessed to his companion on a subsequent occasion that he thought her a little flippant, a little frivolous even for her years. 'Oh yes,' said the girl, on that occasion, 'I have no doubt that you considered she talked too much, for one so old. In America old ladies sit silent and listen to the young.' Mr. Wendover stared a little and replied to this that with her—with Laura Wing—it was impossible to tell which side she was on, the American or the English: sometimes she seemed to take one, sometimes the other. At any rate, he added, smiling, with regard to the other great division it was easy

to see—she was on the side of the old. 'Of course
I am,' she said ; 'when one *is* old !' And then he
inquired, according to his wont, if she were thought
so in England ; to which she answered that it was
England that had made her so.

Lady Davenant's bright drawing-room was
filled with mementoes and especially with a collec-
tion of portraits of distinguished people, mainly
fine old prints with signatures, an array of
precious autographs. 'Oh, it's a cemetery,' she
said, when the young man asked her some
question about one of the pictures ; 'they are my
contemporaries, they are all dead and those things
are the tombstones, with the inscriptions. I'm
the grave-digger, I look after the place and try to
keep it a little tidy. I have dug my own little
hole,' she went on, to Laura, 'and when you are sent
for you must come and put me in.' This evocation
of mortality led Mr. Wendover to ask her if she had
known Charles Lamb ; at which she stared for an
instant, replying: 'Dear me, no—one didn't meet him.'

'Oh, I meant to say Lord Byron,' said Mr.
Wendover.

'Bless me, yes ; I was in love with him. But he
didn't notice me, fortunately—we were so many.
He was very nice-looking but he was very vulgar.'
Lady Davenant talked to Laura as if Mr. Wendover
had not been there ; or rather as if his interests and
knowledge were identical with hers. Before they
went away the young man asked her if she had
known Garrick and she replied : 'Oh, dear, no, we
didn't have them in our houses, in those days.'

'He must have been dead long before you were
born !' Laura exclaimed.

'I daresay ; but one used to hear of him.'

'I think I meant Edmund Kean,' said Mr. Wendover.

'You make little mistakes of a century or two,' Laura Wing remarked, laughing.   She felt now as if she had known Mr. Wendover a long time.

'Oh, he was very clever,' said Lady Davenant.

'Very magnetic, I suppose,' Mr. Wendover went on.

'What's that ?   I believe he used to get tipsy.'

'Perhaps you don't use that expression in England ?' Laura's companion inquired.

'Oh, I daresay we do, if it's American ; we talk American now.   You seem very good-natured people, but such a jargon as you *do* speak !'

'I like *your* way, Lady Davenant,' said Mr. Wendover, benevolently, smiling.

'You might do worse,' cried the old woman ; and then she added : 'Please go out !'   They were taking leave of her but she kept Laura's hand and, for the young man, nodded with decision at the open door. 'Now, wouldn't *he* do ?' she asked, after Mr. Wendover had passed into the hall.

'Do for what ?'

'For a husband, of course.'

'For a husband—for whom ?'

'Why—for me,' said Lady Davenant.

'I don't know—I think he might tire you.'

'Oh—if he's tiresome !' the old lady continued, smiling at the girl.

'I think he is very good,' said Laura.

'Well then, he'll do.'

'Ah, perhaps *you* won't !' Laura exclaimed, smiling back at her and turning away.

VIII

SHE was of a serious turn by nature and unlike many serious people she made no particular study of the art of being gay. Had her circumstances been different she might have done so, but she lived in a merry house (heaven save the mark! as she used to say) and therefore was not driven to amuse herself for conscience sake. The diversions she sought were of a serious cast and she liked those best which showed most the note of difference from Selina's interests and Lionel's. She felt that she was most divergent when she attempted to cultivate her mind, and it was a branch of such cultivation to visit the curiosities, the antiquities, the monuments of London. She was fond of the Abbey and the British Museum—she had extended her researches as far as the Tower. She read the works of Mr. John Timbs and made notes of the old corners of history that had not yet been abolished—the houses in which great men had lived and died. She planned a general tour of inspection of the ancient churches of the City and a pilgrimage to the queer places commemorated by Dickens. It must be added that though her intentions were great her adventures had as yet been small. She had wanted

for opportunity and independence ; people had other
things to do than to go with her, so that it was not
till she had been some time in the country and till
a good while after she had begun to go out alone
that she entered upon the privilege of visiting
public institutions by herself. There were some
aspects of London that frightened her, but there
were certain spots, such as the Poets' Corner in the
Abbey or the room of the Elgin marbles, where she
liked better to be alone than not to have the right
companion. At the time Mr. Wendover presented
himself in Grosvenor Place she had begun to put in,
as they said, a museum or something of that sort
whenever she had a chance. Besides her idea that
such places were sources of knowledge (it is to be
feared that the poor girl's notions of knowledge were
at once conventional and crude) they were also
occasions for detachment, an escape from worrying
thoughts. She forgot Selina and she 'qualified'
herself a little—though for what she hardly knew.

The day Mr. Wendover dined in Grosvenor Place
they talked about St. Paul's, which he expressed a
desire to see, wishing to get some idea of the great
past, as he said, in England as well as of the present.
Laura mentioned that she had spent half an hour the
summer before in the big black temple on Ludgate
Hill ; whereupon he asked her if he might entertain
the hope that—if it were not disagreeable to her to
go again—she would serve as his guide there. She
had taken him to see Lady Davenant, who was so
remarkable and worth a long journey, and now he
should like to pay her back—to show *her* something.
The difficulty would be that there was probably
nothing she had not seen ; but if she could think of

anything he was completely at her service. They sat together at dinner and she told him she would think of something before the repast was over. A little while later she let him know that a charming place had occurred to her—a place to which she was afraid to go alone and where she should be grateful for a protector: she would tell him more about it afterwards. It was then settled between them that on a certain afternoon of the same week they would go to St. Paul's together, extending their ramble as much further as they had time. Laura lowered her voice for this discussion, as if the range of allusion had had a kind of impropriety. She was now still more of the mind that Mr. Wendover was a good young man—he had such worthy eyes. His principal defect was that he treated all subjects as if they were equally important; but that was perhaps better than treating them with equal levity. If one took an interest in him one might not despair of teaching him to discriminate.

Laura said nothing at first to her sister about her appointment with him: the feelings with which she regarded Selina were not such as to make it easy for her to talk over matters of conduct, as it were, with this votary of pleasure at any price, or at any rate to report her arrangements to her as one would do to a person of fine judgment. All the same, as she had a horror of positively hiding anything (Selina herself did that enough for two) it was her purpose to mention at luncheon on the day of the event that she had agreed to accompany Mr. Wendover to St. Paul's. It so happened however that Mrs. Berrington was not at home at this repast; Laura partook of it in the company of Miss Steet and her

young charges. It very often happened now that
the sisters failed to meet in the morning, for Selina
remained very late in her room and there had been
a considerable intermission of the girl's earlier custom
of visiting her there. It was Selina's habit to send
forth from this fragrant sanctuary little hiero-
glyphic notes in which she expressed her wishes or
gave her directions for the day. On the morning I
speak of her maid put into Laura's hand one of these
communications, which contained the words : ' Please
be sure and replace me with the children at lunch—
I meant to give them that hour to-day. But I have
a frantic appeal from Lady Watermouth ; she is
worse and beseeches me to come to her, so I rush for
the 12.30 train.' These lines required no answer
and Laura had no questions to ask about Lady
Watermouth. She knew she was tiresomely ill, in
exile, condemned to forego the diversions of the
season and calling out to her friends, in a house she
had taken for three months at Weybridge (for a
certain particular air) where Selina had already been
to see her. Selina's devotion to her appeared commendable—she had her so much on her mind.
Laura had observed in her sister in relation to other
persons and objects these sudden intensities of charity,
and she had said to herself, watching them—' Is it
because she is bad ?—does she want to make up for
it somehow and to buy herself off from the penalties ?'

Mr. Wendover called for his *cicerone* and they
agreed to go in a romantic, Bohemian manner (the
young man was very docile and appreciative about
this), walking the short distance to the Victoria
station and taking the mysterious underground rail-
way. In the carriage she anticipated the inquiry

that she figured to herself he presently would make
and said, laughing : ' No, no, this is very exceptional ;
if we were both English—and both what we are,
otherwise—we wouldn't do this.'

' And if only one of us were English ? '

' It would depend upon which one.'

' Well, say me.'

' Oh, in that case I certainly—on so short an
acquaintance—would not go sight-seeing with you.'

' Well, I am glad I'm American,' said Mr. Wendover, sitting opposite to her.

' Yes, you may thank your fate.　It's much
simpler,' Laura added.

' Oh, you spoil it ! ' the young man exclaimed—
a speech of which she took no notice but which
made her think him brighter, as they used to say
at home.　He was brighter still after they had descended from the train at the Temple station (they
had meant to go on to Blackfriars, but they jumped
out on seeing the sign of the Temple, fired with the
thought of visiting that institution too) and got ad-
mission to the old garden of the Benchers, which
lies beside the foggy, crowded river, and looked at
the tombs of the crusaders in the low Romanesque
church, with the cross-legged figures sleeping so close
to the eternal uproar, and lingered in the flagged,
homely courts of brick, with their much-lettered
door-posts, their dull old windows and atmosphere
of consultation—lingered to talk of Johnson and
Goldsmith and to remark how London opened one's
eyes to Dickens ; and he was brightest of all when
they stood in the high, bare cathedral, which suggested a dirty whiteness, saying it was fine but
wondering why it was not finer and letting a glance

as cold as the dusty, colourless glass fall upon epi-
taphs that seemed to make most of the defunct
bores even in death.   Mr. Wendover was decorous
but he was increasingly gay, and these qualities
appeared in him in spite of the fact that St. Paul's
was rather a disappointment.   Then they felt the
advantage of having the other place—the one Laura
had had in mind at dinner—to fall back upon : that
perhaps would prove a compensation.   They entered
a hansom now (they had to come to that, though
they had walked also from the Temple to St. Paul's)
and drove to Lincoln's Inn Fields, Laura making
the reflection as they went that it was really a charm
to roam about London under valid protection—such
a mixture of freedom and safety—and that perhaps
she had been unjust, ungenerous to her sister.   A
good-natured, positively charitable doubt came into
her mind—a doubt that Selina might have the
benefit of.   What she liked in her present under-
taking was the element of the *imprévu* that it contained, and perhaps it was simply the same happy
sense of getting the laws of London—once in a way
—off her back that had led Selina to go over to Paris
to ramble about with Captain Crispin.   Possibly
they had done nothing worse than go together to
the Invalides and Notre Dame ; and if any one were
to meet *her* driving that way, so far from home, with
Mr. Wendover—Laura, mentally, did not finish her
sentence, overtaken as she was by the reflection that
she had fallen again into her old assumption (she
had been in and out of it a hundred times), that
Mrs. Berrington *had* met Captain Crispin—the idea
she so passionately repudiated.   She at least would
never deny that she had spent the afternoon with

Mr. Wendover : she would simply say that he was an American and had brought a letter of introduction.

The cab stopped at the Soane Museum, which Laura Wing had always wanted to see, a compatriot having once told her that it was one of the most curious things in London and one of the least known. While Mr. Wendover was discharging the vehicle she looked over the important old-fashioned square (which led her to say to herself that London was endlessly big and one would never know all the places that made it up) and saw a great bank of cloud hanging above it — a definite portent of a summer storm. 'We are going to have thunder ; you had better keep the cab,' she said ; upon which her companion told the man to wait, so that they should not afterwards, in the wet, have to walk for another conveyance. The heterogeneous objects collected by the late Sir John Soane are arranged in a fine old dwelling-house, and the place gives one the impression of a sort of Saturday afternoon of one's youth—a long, rummaging visit, under in-dulgent care, to some eccentric and rather alarming old travelled person. Our young friends wandered from room to room and thought everything queer and some few objects interesting ; Mr. Wendover said it would be a very good place to find a thing you couldn't find anywhere else—it illustrated the prudent virtue of keeping. They took note of the sarcophagi and pagodas, the artless old maps and medals. They admired the fine Hogarths ; there were uncanny, unexpected objects that Laura edged away from, that she would have preferred not to be in the room with. They had been there half an hour—it had grown much darker—when they heard

a tremendous peal of thunder and became aware
that the storm had broken. They watched it a while
from the upper windows—a violent June shower,
with quick sheets of lightning and a rainfall that
danced on the pavements. They took it sociably,
they lingered at the window, inhaling the odour of
the fresh wet that splashed over the sultry town.
They would have to wait till it had passed, and they
resigned themselves serenely to this idea, repeating
very often that it would pass very soon. One of
the keepers told them that there were other rooms
to see—that there were very interesting things in
the basement. They made their way down—it
grew much darker and they heard a great deal of
thunder—and entered a part of the house which
presented itself to Laura as a series of dim, irregular
vaults—passages and little narrow avenues—encum-
bered with strange vague things, obscured for the
time but some of which had a wicked, startling look,
so that she wondered how the keepers could stay
there. 'It's very fearful—it looks like a cave of
idols!' she said to her companion; and then she
added—'Just look there—is that a person or a
thing?' As she spoke they drew nearer to the
object of her reference—a figure in the middle of
a small vista of curiosities, a figure which answered
her question by uttering a short shriek as they ap-
proached. The immediate cause of this cry was
apparently a vivid flash of lightning, which pene-
trated into the room and illuminated both Laura's
face and that of the mysterious person. Our young
lady recognised her sister, as Mrs. Berrington had
evidently recognised her. 'Why, Selina!' broke
from her lips before she had time to check the

words. At the same moment the figure turned
quickly away, and then Laura saw that it was accompanied by another, that of a tall gentleman with
a light beard which shone in the dusk. The two
persons retreated together—dodged out of sight, as
it were, disappearing in the gloom or in the labyrinth
of the objects exhibited. The whole encounter was
but the business of an instant.

'Was it Mrs. Berrington?' Mr. Wendover asked
with interest while Laura stood staring.

'Oh no, I only thought it was at first,' she
managed to reply, very quickly. She had recognised
the gentleman—he had the fine fair beard of Captain
Crispin—and her heart seemed to her to jump up
and down. She was glad her companion could not
see her face, and yet she wanted to get out, to rush
up the stairs, where he would see it again, to
escape from the place. She wished not to be there
with *them*—she was overwhelmed with a sudden
horror. 'She has lied—she has lied again—she
has lied!'—that was the rhythm to which her
thought began to dance. She took a few steps one
way and then another: she was afraid of running
against the dreadful pair again. She remarked to
her companion that it was time they should go off,
and then when he showed her the way back to the
staircase she pleaded that she had not half seen the
things. She pretended suddenly to a deep interest
in them, and lingered there roaming and prying
about. She was flurried still more by the thought
that he would have seen her flurry, and she wondered
whether he believed the woman who had shrieked
and rushed away was *not* Selina. If she was not
Selina why had she shrieked? and if she was Selina

what would Mr. Wendover think of her behaviour,
and of her own, and of the strange accident of their
meeting? What must she herself think of that? so
astonishing it was that in the immensity of London
so infinitesimally small a chance should have got
itself enacted. What a queer place to come to—
for people like them! They would get away as
soon as possible, of that she could be sure; and she
would wait a little to give them time.

Mr. Wendover made no further remark—that
was a relief; though his silence itself seemed to
show that he was mystified. They went upstairs
again and on reaching the door found to their
surprise that their cab had disappeared—a circumstance the more singular as the man had not been
paid. The rain was still coming down, though with
less violence, and the square had been cleared of
vehicles by the sudden storm. The doorkeeper,
perceiving the dismay of our friends, explained that
the cab had been taken up by another lady and
another gentleman who had gone out a few minutes
before; and when they inquired how he had been
induced to depart without the money they owed
him the reply was that there evidently had been a
discussion (he hadn't heard it, but the lady seemed
in a fearful hurry) and the gentleman had told him
that they would make it all up to him and give him
a lot more into the bargain. The doorkeeper
hazarded the candid surmise that the cabby would
make ten shillings by the job. But there were plenty
more cabs; there would be one up in a minute and
the rain moreover was going to stop. 'Well, that *is*
sharp practice!' said Mr. Wendover. He made no·
further allusion to the identity of the lady.

IX

THE rain did stop while they stood there, and a
brace of hansoms was not slow to appear. Laura
told her companion that he must put her into one—
she could go home alone : she had taken up enough
of his time. He deprecated this course very respectfully ; urged that he had it on his conscience to
deliver her at her own door ; but she sprang into
the cab and closed the apron with a movement that
was a sharp prohibition. She wanted to get away
from him—it would be too awkward, the long,
pottering drive back. Her hansom started off
while Mr. Wendover, smiling sadly, lifted his hat.
It was not very comfortable, even without him ;
especially as before she had gone a quarter of a mile
she felt that her action had been too marked—she
wished she had let him come. His puzzled, innocent
air of wondering what was the matter annoyed her ;
and she was in the absurd situation of being angry
at a desistence which she would have been still
angrier if he had been guiltless of. It would have
comforted her (because it would seem to share her
burden) and yet it would have covered her with
shame if he had guessed that what she saw was
wrong. It would not occur to him that there was a

scandal so near her, because he thought with no
great promptitude of such things ; and yet, since
there was—but since there was after all Laura
scarcely knew what attitude would sit upon him
most gracefully.   As to what he might be prepared
to suspect by having heard what Selina's reputation
was in London, of that Laura was unable to judge,
not knowing what was said, because of course it was
not said to *her*.   Lionel would undertake to give her
the benefit of this any moment she would allow him,
but how in the world could *he* know either, for how
could things be said to him ?   Then, in the rattle
of the hansom, passing through streets for which
the girl had no eyes, 'She has lied, she has
lied, she has lied !' kept repeating itself.   Why
had she written and signed that wanton falsehood
about her going down to Lady Watermouth ?   How
could she have gone to Lady Watermouth's when she
was making so very different and so extraordinary a
use of the hours she had announced her intention of
spending there ?   What had been the need of that
misrepresentation and why did she lie before she
was driven to it ?

It was because she was false altogether and
deception came out of her with her breath ; she was
so depraved that it was easier to her to fabricate
than to let it alone.   Laura would not have asked
her to give an account of her day, but she would
ask her now.   She shuddered at one moment, as
she found herself saying—even in silence—such
things of her sister, and the next she sat staring out
of the front of the cab at the stiff problem presented
by Selina's turning up with the partner of her guilt
at the Soane Museum, of all places in the world.

The girl shifted this fact about in various ways, to account for it—not unconscious as she did so that it was a pretty exercise of ingenuity for a nice girl. Plainly, it was a rare accident: if it had been their plan to spend the day together the Soane Museum had not been in the original programme. They had been near it, they had been on foot and they had rushed in to take refuge from the rain. But how did they come to be near it and above all to be on foot? How could Selina do anything so reckless from her own point of view as to walk about the town—even an out-of-the-way part of it—with her suspected lover? Laura Wing felt the want of proper knowledge to explain such anomalies. It was too little clear to her where ladies went and how they proceeded when they consorted with gentlemen in regard to their meetings with whom they had to lie. She knew nothing of where Captain Crispin lived; very possibly—for she vaguely remembered having heard Selina say of him that he was very poor—he had chambers in that part of the town, and they were either going to them or coming from them. If Selina had neglected to take her way in a four-wheeler with the glasses up it was through some chance that would not seem natural till it was explained, like that of their having darted into a public institution. Then no doubt it would hang together with the rest only too well. The explanation most exact would probably be that the pair had snatched a walk together (in the course of a day of many edifying episodes) for the 'lark' of it, and for the sake of the walk had taken the risk, which in that part of London, so detached from all gentility, had appeared to them small. The last

thing Selina could have expected was to meet her
sister in such a strange corner—her sister with a
young man of her own!

She was dining out that night with both Selina
and Lionel—a conjunction that was rather rare.
She was by no means always invited with them,
and Selina constantly went without her husband.
Appearances, however, sometimes got a sop thrown
them; three or four times a month Lionel and she
entered the brougham together like people who still
had forms, who still said 'my dear.' This was to
be one of those occasions, and Mrs. Berrington's
young unmarried sister was included in the invitation. When Laura reached home she learned, on
inquiry, that Selina had not yet come in, and she
went straight to her own room. If her sister had
been there she would have gone to hers instead—
she would have cried out to her as soon as she had
closed the door: 'Oh, stop, stop—in God's name,
stop before you go any further, before exposure and
ruin and shame come down and bury us!' That
was what was in the air—the vulgarest disgrace,
and the girl, harder now than ever about her sister,
was conscious of a more passionate desire to save
herself. But Selina's absence made the difference
that during the next hour a certain chill fell upon
this impulse from other feelings: she found suddenly that she was late and she began to dress.
They were to go together after dinner to a couple of
balls; a diversion which struck her as ghastly for
people who carried such horrors in their breasts.
Ghastly was the idea of the drive of husband, wife
and sister in pursuit of pleasure, with falsity and
detection and hate between them. Selina's maid

came to her door to tell her that she was in the
carriage—an extraordinary piece of punctuality, which
made her wonder, as Selina was always dreadfully
late for everything.   Laura went down as quickly as
she could, passed through the open door, where the
servants were grouped in the foolish majesty of their
superfluous attendance, and through the file of dingy
gazers who had paused at the sight of the carpet
across the pavement and the waiting carriage, in
which Selina sat in pure white splendour.   Mrs.
Berrington had a tiara on her head and a proud
patience in her face, as if her sister were really a
sore trial.   As soon as the girl had taken her place
she said to the footman : ' Is Mr. Berrington there ? '
—to which the man replied : ' No ma'am, not
yet.'   It was not new to Laura that if there was
any one later as a general thing than Selina it was
Selina's husband.   ' Then he must take a hansom.
Go on.'   The footman mounted and they rolled
away.

There were several different things that had been
present to Laura's mind during the last couple of
hours as destined to mark—one or the other—this
present encounter with her sister ; but the words
Selina spoke the moment the brougham began to move
were of course exactly those she had not foreseen.
She had considered that she might take this tone or
that tone or even no tone at all ; she was quite prepared for her presenting a face of blankness to any
form of interrogation and saying, ' What on earth
are you talking about ? '   It was in short conceivable
to her that Selina would deny absolutely that she
had been in the museum, that they had stood face to
face and that she had fled in confusion.   She was cap-

able of explaining the incident by an idiotic error
on Laura's part, by her having seized on another
person, by her seeing Captain Crispin in every
bush; though doubtless she would be taxed (of
course she would say *that* was the woman's own
affair) to supply a reason for the embarrassment of
the other lady. But she was not prepared for
Selina's breaking out with : ' Will you be so good as
to inform me if you are engaged to be married to
Mr. Wendover ? '

' Engaged to him ? I have seen him but three
times.'

' And is that what you usually do with gentlemen
you have seen three times ? '

' Are you talking about my having gone with him
to see some sights ? I see nothing wrong in that.
To begin with you see what he is. One might
go with him anywhere. Then he brought us an
introduction—we have to do something for him.
Moreover you threw him upon me the moment he
came—you asked me to take charge of him.'

' I didn't ask you to be indecent ! If Lionel were
to know it he wouldn't tolerate it, so long as you live
with us.'

Laura was silent a moment. ' I shall not live
with you long.' The sisters, side by side, with their
heads turned, looked at each other, a deep crimson
leaping into Laura's face. ' I wouldn't have believed
it—that you are so bad,' she said. ' You are horrible ! ' She saw that Selina had not taken up the
idea of denying—she judged that would be hope-
less : the recognition on either side had been too
sharp. She looked radiantly handsome, especially
with the strange new expression that Laura's last

word brought into her eyes. This expression seemed
to the girl to show her more of Selina morally
than she had ever yet seen—something of the full
extent and the miserable limit.

'It's different for a married woman, especially
when she's married to a cad. It's in a girl that such
things are odious—scouring London with strange
men. I am not bound to explain to you—there
would be too many things to say. I have my
reasons—I have my conscience. It was the oddest
of all things, our meeting in that place—I know that
as well as you,' Selina went on, with her wonderful
affected clearness; 'but it was not your finding me
that was out of the way; it was my finding you—
with your remarkable escort! That was incredible.
I pretended not to recognise you, so that the gentleman who was with me shouldn't see you, shouldn't
know you. He questioned me and I repudiated you.
You may thank me for saving you! You had better
wear a veil next time—one never knows what may
happen. I met an acquaintance at Lady Watermouth's and he came up to town with me. He
happened to talk about old prints; I told him how
I have collected them and we spoke of the bother
one has about the frames. He insisted on my going
with him to that place—from Waterloo—to see such
an excellent model.'

Laura had turned her face to the window of the
carriage again; they were spinning along Park Lane,
passing in the quick flash of other vehicles an end-
less succession of ladies with 'dressed' heads, of
gentlemen in white neckties. 'Why, I thought your
frames were all so pretty!' Laura murmured. Then
she added: 'I suppose it was your eagerness to save

your companion the shock of seeing me—in my
dishonour—that led you to steal our cab.'

'Your cab?'

'Your delicacy was expensive for you!'

'You don't mean you were knocking about in
cabs with him!' Selina cried.

'Of course I know that you don't really think
a word of what you say about me,' Laura went on;
'though I don't know that that makes your saying
it a bit less unspeakably base.'

The brougham pulled up in Park Lane and Mrs.
Berrington bent herself to have a view through the
front glass. 'We are there, but there are two other
carriages,' she remarked, for all answer. 'Ah, there
are the Collingwoods.'

'Where are you going—where are you going—
where are you going?' Laura broke out.

The carriage moved on, to set them down, and
while the footman was getting off the box Selina
said: 'I don't pretend to be better than other women,
but you do!' And being on the side of the house
she quickly stepped out and carried her crowned
brilliancy through the long-lingering daylight and
into the open portals.

X

'What do you intend to do? You will grant that I have a right to ask you that.'

'To do? I shall do as I have always done—not so badly, as it seems to me.'

This colloquy took place in Mrs. Berrington's room, in the early morning hours, after Selina's return from the entertainment to which reference was last made. Her sister came home before her—she found herself incapable of 'going on' when Selina quitted the house in Park Lane at which they had dined. Mrs. Berrington had the night still before her, and she stepped into her carriage with her usual air of graceful resignation to a brilliant lot. She had taken the precaution, however, to provide herself with a defence, against a little sister bristling with righteousness, in the person of Mrs. Collingwood, to whom she offered a lift, as they were bent upon the same business and Mr. Collingwood had a use of his own for his brougham. The Collingwoods were a happy pair who could discuss such a divergence before their friends candidly, amicably, with a great many 'My loves' and 'Not for the worlds.' Lionel Berrington disappeared after dinner, without holding any communication with his wife, and Laura ex-

pected to find that he had taken the carriage, to
repay her in kind for her having driven off from
Grosvenor Place without him. But it was not new
to the girl that he really spared his wife more than
she spared him ; not so much perhaps because he
wouldn't do the 'nastiest' thing as because he
couldn't. Selina could always be nastier. There
was ever a whimsicality in her actions : if two or
three hours before it had been her fancy to keep a
third person out of the carriage she had now her
reasons for bringing such a person in. Laura knew
that she would not only pretend, but would really
believe, that her vindication of her conduct on their
way to dinner had been powerful and that she had
won a brilliant victory. What need, therefore, to
thresh out further a subject that she had chopped
into atoms ? Laura Wing, however, had needs of
her own, and her remaining in the carriage when the
footman next opened the door was intimately connected with them.

'I don't care to go in,' she said to her sister. 'If
you will allow me to be driven home and send back
the carriage for you, that's what I shall like best.'

Selina stared and Laura knew what she would
have said if she could have spoken her thought.
'Oh, you are furious that I haven't given you a
chance to fly at me again, and you must take it out
in sulks !' These were the ideas—ideas of 'fury'
and sulks—into which Selina could translate feelings
that sprang from the pure depths of one's conscience.
Mrs. Collingwood protested—she said it was a shame
that Laura shouldn't go in and enjoy herself when
she looked so lovely. 'Doesn't she look lovely ?'
She appealed to Mrs. Berrington. 'Bless us, what's

the use of being pretty? Now, if she had *my* face!'

'I think she looks rather cross,' said Selina, getting out with her friend and leaving her sister to her own inventions. Laura had a vision, as the carriage drove away again, of what her situation would have been, or her peace of mind, if Selina and Lionel had been good, attached people like the Collingwoods, and at the same time of the singularity of a good woman's being ready to accept favours from a person as to whose behaviour she had the lights that must have come to the lady in question in regard to Selina. She accepted favours herself and she only wanted to be good : that was oppressively true ; but if she had not been Selina's sister she would never drive in her carriage. That conviction was strong in the girl as this vehicle conveyed her to Grosvenor Place ; but it was not in its nature consoling. The prevision of disgrace was now so vivid to her that it seemed to her that if it had not already overtaken them she had only to thank the loose, mysterious, rather ignoble tolerance of people like Mrs. Collingwood. There were plenty of that species, even among the good ; perhaps indeed exposure and dishonour would begin only when the bad had got hold of the facts. Would the bad be most horrified and do most to spread the scandal? There were, in any event, plenty of them too.

Laura sat up for her sister that night, with that nice question to help her to torment herself—whether if she was hard and merciless in judging Selina it would be with the bad too that she would associate herself. Was she all wrong after all—was she cruel by being too rigid? Was Mrs. Collingwood's attitude the right one and ought she only to propose to herself to 'allow' more and more, and to allow ever, and to smooth things down by gentleness, by sympathy, by not looking at them too hard? It was not the first time that the just measure of things seemed to slip from her hands as she became conscious of possible, or rather of very actual, differences of standard and usage. On this occasion Geordie and Ferdy asserted themselves, by the mere force of lying asleep upstairs in their little cribs, as on the whole the proper measure. Laura went into the nursery to look at them when she came home—it was her habit almost any night—and yearned over them as mothers and maids do alike over the pillow of rosy childhood. They were an antidote to all casuistry; for Selina to forget *them*—that was the beginning and the end of shame. She came back to the library, where she should best hear the sound of her sister's return; the hours passed as she sat there, without bringing round this event. Carriages came and went all night; the soft shock of swift hoofs was on the wooden roadway long after the summer dawn grew fair—till it was merged in the rumble of the awakening day. Lionel had not come in when she returned, and he continued absent, to Laura's satisfaction; for if she wanted not to miss Selina she had no desire at present to have to tell her brother-in-law why she was sitting up. She prayed Selina might arrive first: then she would have more time to think of something that harassed her particularly—the question of whether she ought to tell Lionel that she had seen her in a far-away corner of the town with Captain Crispin. Almost impossible as she found it now to feel any tenderness

for her, she yet detested the idea of bearing witness
against her : notwithstanding which it appeared to
her that she could make up her mind to do this if
there were a chance of its preventing the last scandal
—a catastrophe to which she saw her sister rushing straight.   That Selina was capable at a given
moment of going off with her lover, and capable of
it precisely because it was the greatest ineptitude as
well as the greatest wickedness—there was a voice
of prophecy, of warning, to this effect in the silent,
empty house.   If repeating to Lionel what she had
seen would contribute to prevent anything, or to
stave off the danger, was it not her duty to denounce
his wife, flesh and blood of her own as she was, to
his further reprobation ?   This point was not intolerably difficult to determine, as she sat there waiting,
only because even what was righteous in that reprobation could not present itself to her as fruitful or
efficient.   What could Lionel frustrate, after all, and
what intelligent or authoritative step was he capable
of taking ?   Mixed with all that now haunted her
was her consciousness of what his own absence at
such an hour represented in the way of the unedi-
fying.   He might be at some sporting club or he
might be anywhere else ; at any rate he was not
where he ought to be at three o'clock in the morning.   Such the husband such the wife, she said to
herself ; and she felt that Selina would have a kind
of advantage, which she grudged her, if she should
come in and say : ' And where is *he*, please—where
is he, the exalted being on whose behalf you have
undertaken to preach so much better than he himself
practises ? '

But still Selina failed to come in—even to take

that advantage ; yet in proportion as her waiting
was useless did the girl find it impossible to go to
bed.   A new fear had seized her, the fear that she
would never come back at all—that they were already
in the presence of the dreaded catastrophe.   This
made her so nervous that she paced about the lower
rooms, listening to every sound, roaming till she was
tired.   She knew it was absurd, the image of Selina
taking flight in a ball-dress ; but she said to herself
that she might very well have sent other clothes
away, in advance, somewhere (Laura had her own
ripe views about the maid) ; and at any rate, for
herself, that was the fate she had to expect, if not
that night then some other one soon, and it was all
the same : to sit counting the hours till a hope was
given up and a hideous certainty remained.   She
had fallen into such a state of apprehension that
when at last she heard a carriage stop at the door
she was almost happy, in spite of her prevision of
how disgusted her sister would be to find her.   They
met in the hall—Laura went out as she heard the
opening of the door.   Selina stopped short, seeing
her, but said nothing—on account apparently of the
presence of the sleepy footman.   Then she moved
straight to the stairs, where she paused again, asking
the footman if Mr. Berrington had come in.

'Not yet, ma'am,' the footman answered.

'Ah !' said Mrs. Berrington, dramatically, and
ascended the stairs.

'I have sat up on purpose—I want particularly
to speak to you,' Laura remarked, following her.

'Ah !' Selina repeated, more superior still.   She
went fast, almost as if she wished to get to her
room before her sister could overtake her.   But the

girl was close behind her, she passed into the room
with her.   Laura closed the door ; then she told
her that she had found it impossible to go to bed
without asking her what she intended to do.

'Your behaviour is too monstrous !' Selina flashed
out.   'What on earth do you wish to make the
servants suppose ? '

'Oh, the servants——in *this* house ; as if one could
put any idea into their heads that is not there
already !' Laura thought.   But she said nothing
of this——she only repeated her question : aware that
she was exasperating to her sister but also aware
that she could not be anything else.   Mrs. Berrington, whose maid, having outlived surprises, had
gone to rest, began to divest herself of some of her
ornaments, and it was not till after a moment, during which she stood before the glass, that she made
that answer about doing as she had always done.
To this Laura rejoined that she ought to put herself
in her place enough to feel how important it was to
her to know what was likely to happen, so that she
might take time by the forelock and think of her
own situation.   If anything should happen she would
infinitely rather be out of it——be as far away as
possible.   Therefore she must take her measures.

It was in the mirror that they looked at each
other——in the strange, candle-lighted duplication of
the scene that their eyes met.   Selina drew the
diamonds out of her hair, and in this occupation,
for a minute, she was silent.   Presently she asked :
'What are you talking about——what do you allude
to as happening ? '

'Why, it seems to me that there is nothing left
for you but to go away with him.   If there is a

prospect of that insanity——' But here Laura
stopped ; something so unexpected was taking place
in Selina's countenance—the movement that pre-
cedes a sudden gush of tears. Mrs. Berrington
dashed down the glittering pins she had detached
from her tresses, and the next moment she had flung
herself into an armchair and was weeping profusely,
extravagantly. Laura forbore to go to her ; she
made no motion to soothe or reassure her, she only
stood and watched her tears and wondered what
they signified. Somehow even the slight refresh-
ment she felt at having affected her in that particular and, as it had lately come to seem, improbable
way did not suggest to her that they were precious
symptoms. Since she had come to disbelieve her
word so completely there was nothing precious about
Selina any more. But she continued for some
moments to cry passionately, and while this lasted
Laura remained silent. At last from the midst of
her sobs Selina broke out, 'Go away, go away—
leave me alone !'

'Of course I infuriate you,' said the girl ; 'but
how can I see you rush to your ruin—to that of all
of us—without holding on to you and dragging you
back ?'

'Oh, you don't understand anything about anything !' Selina wailed, with her beautiful hair tumbling
all over her.

'I certainly don't understand how you can give
such a tremendous handle to Lionel.'

At the mention of her husband's name Selina
always gave a bound, and she sprang up now,
shaking back her dense braids. 'I give him no
handle and you don't know what you are talking

about ! I know what I am doing and what becomes
me, and I don't care if I do. He is welcome to all
the handles in the world, for all that he can do with
them !'

'In the name of common pity think of your
children !' said Laura.

'Have I ever thought of anything else ? Have
you sat up all night to have the pleasure of accusing
me of cruelty ? Are there sweeter or more delightful children in the world, and isn't that a little *my*
merit, pray ?' Selina went on, sweeping away her
tears. 'Who has made them what they are, pray ?
—is it their lovely father ? Perhaps you'll say it's
you ! Certainly you have been nice to them, but
you must remember that you only came here the
other day. Isn't it only for them that I am trying
to keep myself alive ?'

This formula struck Laura Wing as grotesque, so
that she replied with a laugh which betrayed too
much her impression, 'Die for them—that would be
better !'

Her sister, at this, looked at her with an extraordinary cold gravity. 'Don't interfere between me
and my children. And for God's sake cease to
harry me !'

Laura turned away : she said to herself that, given
that intensity of silliness, of course the worst would
come. She felt sick and helpless, and, practically,
she had got the certitude she both wanted and
dreaded. 'I don't know what has become of your
mind,' she murmured ; and she went to the door.
But before she reached it Selina had flung herself upon her in one of her strange but, as she felt,
really not encouraging revulsions. Her arms were

about her, she clung to her, she covered Laura with
the tears that had again begun to flow.   She be-
sought her to save her, to stay with her, to help her
against herself, against *him*, against Lionel, against
everything—to forgive her also all the horrid things
she had said to her.   Mrs. Berrington melted, liquefied,
and the room was deluged with her repentance, her
desolation, her confession, her promises and the articles
of apparel which were detached from her by the high
tide of her agitation.   Laura remained with her for
an hour, and before they separated the culpable
woman had taken a tremendous vow — kneeling
before her sister with her head in her lap—never
again, as long as she lived, to consent to see Captain
Crispin or to address a word to him, spoken or
written.   The girl went terribly tired to bed.

A month afterwards she lunched with Lady Davenant, whom she had not seen since the day she
took Mr. Wendover to call upon her.   The old
woman had found herself obliged to entertain a
small company, and as she disliked set parties she
sent Laura a request for sympathy and assistance.
She had disencumbered herself, at the end of so
many years, of the burden of hospitality ; but every
now and then she invited people, in order to prove
that she was not too old.   Laura suspected her of
choosing stupid ones on purpose to prove it better—
to show that she could submit not only to the extraordinary but, what was much more difficult, to the
usual.   But when they had been properly fed she
encouraged them to disperse ; on this occasion as
the party broke up Laura was the only person she
asked to stay.   She wished to know in the first place
why she had not been to see her for so long, and in

the second how that young man had behaved—the
one she had brought that Sunday.   Lady Davenant
didn't remember his name, though he had been so
good-natured, as she said, since then, as to leave a
card.   If he had behaved well that was a very good
reason for the girl's neglect and Laura need give no
other.   Laura herself would not have behaved well
if at such a time she had been running after old
women.   There was nothing, in general, that the
girl liked less than being spoken of, off-hand, as a
marriageable article—being planned and arranged
for in this particular.   It made too light of her
independence, and though in general such inventions
passed for benevolence they had always seemed to
her to contain at bottom an impertinence—as if
people could be moved about like a game of
chequers.   There was a liberty in the way Lady
Davenant's imagination disposed of her (with such
an *insouciance* of her own preferences), but she for-
gave that, because after all this old friend was not
obliged to think of her at all.

'I knew that you were almost always out of
town now, on Sundays—and so have we been,'
Laura said.   'And then I have been a great deal
with my sister—more than before.'

'More than before what?'

'Well, a kind of estrangement we had, about a
certain matter.'

'And now you have made it all up?'

'Well, we have been able to talk of it (we
couldn't before—without painful scenes), and that
has cleared the air.   We have gone about together a
good deal,' Laura went on.   'She has wanted me
constantly with her.'

'That's very nice. And where has she taken
you?' asked the old lady.

'Oh, it's I who have taken her, rather.' And
Laura hesitated.

'Where do you mean?—to say her prayers?'

'Well, to some concerts—and to the National
Gallery.'

Lady Davenant laughed, disrespectfully, at this,
and the girl watched her with a mournful face.
'My dear child, you are too delightful! You are
trying to reform her? by Beethoven and Bach, by
Rubens and Titian?'

'She is very intelligent, about music and pictures
—she has excellent ideas,' said Laura.

'And you have been trying to draw them out?
that is very commendable.'

'I think you are laughing at me, but I don't care,'
the girl declared, smiling faintly.

'Because you have a consciousness of success?—
in what do they call it?—the attempt to raise her
tone? You have been trying to wind her up, and
you *have* raised her tone?'

'Oh, Lady Davenant, I don't know and I don't
understand!' Laura broke out. 'I don't understand
anything any more—I have given up trying.'

'That's what I recommended you to do last winter.
Don't you remember that day at Plash?'

'You told me to let her go,' said Laura.

'And evidently you haven't taken my advice.'

'How can I—how can I?'

'Of course, how can you? And meanwhile if
she doesn't go it's so much gained. But even if
she should, won't that nice young man remain?'
Lady Davenant inquired. 'I hope very much

Selina hasn't taken you altogether away from him.'

Laura was silent a moment; then she returned: 'What nice young man would ever look at me, if anything bad should happen?'

'I would never look at *him* if he should let that prevent him!' the old woman cried. 'It isn't for your sister he loves you, I suppose; is it?'

'He doesn't love me at all.'

'Ah, then he does?' Lady Davenant demanded, with some eagerness, laying her hand on the girl's arm. Laura sat near her on her sofa and looked at her, for all answer to this, with an expression of which the sadness appeared to strike the old woman freshly. 'Doesn't he come to the house—doesn't he say anything?' she continued, with a voice of kindness.

'He comes to the house—very often.'

'And don't you like him?'

'Yes, very much—more than I did at first.'

'Well, as you liked him at first well enough to bring him straight to see me, I suppose that means that now you are immensely pleased with him.'

'He's a gentleman,' said Laura.

'So he seems to me. But why then doesn't he speak out?'

'Perhaps that's the very reason! Seriously,' the girl added, 'I don't know what he comes to the house for.'

'Is he in love with your sister?'

'I sometimes think so.'

'And does she encourage him?'

'She detests him.'

'Oh, then, I like him! I shall immediately

write to him to come and see me : I shall appoint an hour and give him a piece of my mind.'

'If I believed that, I should kill myself,' said Laura.

'You may believe what you like ; but I wish you didn't show your feelings so in your eyes. They might be those of a poor widow with fifteen children. When I was young I managed to be happy, whatever occurred ; and I am sure I looked so.'

'Oh yes, Lady Davenant—for you it was different. You were safe, in so many ways,' Laura said. 'And you were surrounded with consideration.'

'I don't know ; some of us were very wild, and exceedingly ill thought of, and I didn't cry about it. However, there are natures and natures. If you will come and stay with me to-morrow I will take you in.'

'You know how kind I think you, but I have promised Selina not to leave her.'

'Well, then, if she keeps you she must at least go straight !' cried the old woman, with some asperity. Laura made no answer to this and Lady Davenant asked, after a moment : 'And what is Lionel doing ?'

'I don't know—he is very quiet.'

'Doesn't it please him—his wife's improvement ?' The girl got up ; apparently she was made uncomfortable by the ironical effect, if not by the ironical intention, of this question. Her old friend was kind but she was penetrating ; her very next words pierced further. 'Of course if you are really protecting her I can't count upon you' : a remark not adapted to enliven Laura, who would have liked immensely to transfer herself to Queen's Gate and had her very private ideas as to the efficacy of her

protection.   Lady Davenant kissed her and then
suddenly said—'Oh, by the way, his address ; you
must tell me that.'

'His address ?'

'The young man's whom you brought here.
But it's no matter,' the old woman added ; 'the
butler will have entered it—from his card.'

'Lady Davenant, you won't do anything so
loathsome !' the girl cried, seizing her hand.

'Why is it loathsome, if he comes so often ?
It's rubbish, his caring for Selina—a married woman
—when you are there.'

'Why is it rubbish—when so many other people
do ?'

'Oh, well, he is different—I could see that ; or if
he isn't he ought to be !'

'He likes to observe—he came here to take
notes,' said the girl.   'And he thinks Selina a very
interesting London specimen.'

'In spite of her dislike of him ?'

'Oh, he doesn't know that !' Laura exclaimed.

'Why not ? he isn't a fool.'

'Oh, I have made it seem——' But here Laura
stopped ; her colour had risen.

Lady Davenant stared an instant.   'Made it seem
that she inclines to him ?   Mercy, to do that how
fond of him you must be !'   An observation which
had the effect of driving the girl straight out of the
house.

ON one of the last days of June Mrs. Berrington showed her sister a note she had received from 'your dear friend,' as she called him, Mr. Wendover. This was the manner in which she usually designated him, but she had naturally, in the present phase of her relations with Laura, never indulged in any renewal of the eminently perverse insinuations by means of which she had attempted, after the incident at the Soane Museum, to throw dust in her eyes. Mr. Wendover proposed to Mrs. Berrington that she and her sister should honour with their presence a box he had obtained for the opera three nights later—an occasion of high curiosity, the first appearance of a young American singer of whom considerable things were expected. Laura left it to Selina to decide whether they should accept this invitation, and Selina proved to be of two or three differing minds. First she said it wouldn't be convenient to her to go, and she wrote to the young man to this effect. Then, on second thoughts, she considered she might very well go, and telegraphed an acceptance. Later she saw reason to regret her acceptance and communicated this circumstance to her sister, who remarked that it was still not too late

to change. Selina left her in ignorance till the
next day as to whether she had retracted; then
she told her that she had let the matter stand—
they would go. To this Laura replied that she
was glad—for Mr. Wendover. 'And for yourself,'
Selina said, leaving the girl to wonder why every
one (this universality was represented by Mrs.
Lionel Berrington and Lady Davenant) had taken
up the idea that she entertained a passion for her
compatriot. She was clearly conscious that this
was not the case; though she was glad her esteem
for him had not yet suffered the disturbance of her
seeing reason to believe that Lady Davenant had
already meddled, according to her terrible threat.
Laura was surprised to learn afterwards that Selina
had, in London parlance, 'thrown over' a dinner in
order to make the evening at the opera fit in. The
dinner would have made her too late, and she
didn't care about it: she wanted to hear the whole
opera.

The sisters dined together alone, without any
question of Lionel, and on alighting at Covent
Garden found Mr. Wendover awaiting them in the
portico. His box proved commodious and comfortable, and Selina was gracious to him: she thanked
him for his consideration in not stuffing it full of
people. He assured her that he expected but one
other inmate—a gentleman of a shrinking disposition, who would take up no room. The gentleman
came in after the first act; he was introduced to
the ladies as Mr. Booker, of Baltimore. He knew
a great deal about the young lady they had come to
listen to, and he was not so shrinking but that he
attempted to impart a portion of his knowledge

even while she was singing.   Before the second
act was over Laura perceived Lady Ringrose in a
box on the other side of the house, accompanied by
a lady unknown to her.   There was apparently
another person in the box, behind the two ladies,
whom they turned round from time to time to talk
with.   Laura made no observation about Lady
Ringrose to her sister, and she noticed that Selina
never resorted to the glass to look at her.   That
Mrs. Berrington had not failed to see her, however,
was proved by the fact that at the end of the
second act (the opera was Meyerbeer's *Huguenots*)
she suddenly said, turning to Mr. Wendover : ' I
hope you won't mind very much if I go for a short
time to sit with a friend on the other side of the
house.'   She smiled with all her sweetness as she
announced this intention, and had the benefit of
the fact that an apologetic expression is highly
becoming to a pretty woman.   But she abstained
from looking at her sister, and the latter, after
a wondering glance at her, looked at Mr. Wendover.
She saw that he was disappointed—even slightly
wounded : he had taken some trouble to get his
box and it had been no small pleasure to him to
see it graced by the presence of a celebrated beauty.
Now his situation collapsed if the celebrated beauty
were going to transfer her light to another quarter.
Laura was unable to imagine what had come into
her sister's head—to make her so inconsiderate, so
rude.   Selina tried to perform her act of defection
in a soothing, conciliating way, so far as appealing
eyebeams went ; but she gave no particular reason
for her escapade, withheld the name of the friends
in question and betrayed no consciousness that it

was not usual for ladies to roam about the lobbies.
Laura asked her no question, but she said to her,
after an hesitation : ' You won't be long, surely.
You know you oughtn't to leave me here.' Selina
took no notice of this—excused herself in no way
to the girl. Mr. Wendover only exclaimed, smiling
in reference to Laura's last remark : ' Oh, so far as
leaving you here goes——!' In spite of his great
defect (and it was his only one, that she could see)
of having only an ascending scale of seriousness, she
judged him interestedly enough to feel a real pleasure in noticing that though he was annoyed at
Selina's going away and not saying that she would
come back soon, he conducted himself as a gentleman should, submitted respectfully, gallantly, to
her wish. He suggested that her friends might
perhaps, instead, be induced to come to his box, but
when she had objected, ' Oh, you see, there are too
many,' he put her shawl on her shoulders, opened
the box, offered her his arm. While this was going
on Laura saw Lady Ringrose studying them with her
glass. Selina refused Mr. Wendover's arm ; she said,
'Oh no, you stay with *her*—I daresay *he'll* take me :'
and she gazed inspiringly at Mr. Booker. Selina
never mentioned a name when the pronoun would
do. Mr. Booker of course sprang to the service
required and led her away, with an injunction from
his friend to bring her back promptly. As they
went off Laura heard Selina say to her companion
—and she knew Mr. Wendover could also hear it—
' Nothing would have induced me to leave her alone
with *you !*' She thought this a very extraordinary
speech — she thought it even vulgar ; especially
considering that she had never seen the young

man till half an hour before and since then had
not exchanged twenty words with him. It came to
their ears so distinctly that Laura was moved to
notice it by exclaiming, with a laugh : 'Poor Mr.
Booker, what does she suppose I would do to
him ?'

'Oh, it's for you she's afraid,' said Mr. Wendover.

Laura went on, after a moment : 'She oughtn't
to have left me alone with you, either.'

'Oh yes, she ought—after all !' the young man
returned.

The girl had uttered these words from no desire
to say something flirtatious, but because they simply
expressed a part of the judgment she passed, mentally, on Selina's behaviour. She had a sense of
wrong—of being made light of ; for Mrs. Berrington
certainly knew that honourable women didn't (for
the appearance of the thing) arrange to leave their
unmarried sister sitting alone, publicly, at the play-
house, with a couple of young men—the couple that
there would be as soon as Mr. Booker should come
back. It displeased her that the people in the
opposite box, the people Selina had joined, should
see her exhibited in this light. She drew the curtain
of the box a little, she moved a little more behind
it, and she heard her companion utter a vague appealing, protecting sigh, which seemed to express
his sense (her own corresponded with it) that the
glory of the occasion had somehow suddenly departed. At the end of some minutes she perceived
among Lady Ringrose and her companions a movement which appeared to denote that Selina had
come in. The two ladies in front turned round—
something went on at the back of the box. 'She's

there,' Laura said, indicating the place; but Mrs.
Berrington did not show herself — she remained
masked by the others. Neither was Mr. Booker
visible; he had not, seemingly, been persuaded to
remain, and indeed Laura could see that there would
not have been room for him. Mr. Wendover observed, ruefully, that as Mrs. Berrington evidently
could see nothing at all from where she had gone
she had exchanged a very good place for a very bad
one. 'I can't imagine—I can't imagine——' said
the girl; but she paused, losing herself in reflections
and wonderments, in conjectures that soon became
anxieties. Suspicion of Selina was now so rooted
in her heart that it could make her unhappy even
when it pointed nowhere, and by the end of half an
hour she felt how little her fears had really been
lulled since that scene of dishevelment and contrition
in the early dawn.

The opera resumed its course, but Mr. Booker
did not come back. The American singer trilled
and warbled, executed remarkable flights, and there
was much applause, every symptom of success; but
Laura became more and more unaware of the music
—she had no eyes but for Lady Ringrose and her
friend. She watched them earnestly—she tried to
sound with her glass the curtained dimness behind
them. Their attention was all for the stage and
they gave no present sign of having any fellow-
listeners. These others had either gone away or
were leaving them very much to themselves. Laura
was unable to guess any particular motive on her
sister's part, but the conviction grew within her that
she had not put such an affront on Mr. Wendover
simply in order to have a little chat with Lady

Ringrose. There was something else, there was
some one else, in the affair; and when once the
girl's idea had become as definite as that it took
but little longer to associate itself with the image
of Captain Crispin. This image made her draw
back further behind her curtain, because it brought
the blood to her face; and if she coloured for shame
she coloured also for anger. Captain Crispin was
there, in the opposite box; those horrible women
concealed him (she forgot how harmless and well-
read Lady Ringrose had appeared to her that time
at Mellows); they had lent themselves to this
abominable proceeding. Selina was nestling there
in safety with him, by their favour, and she had had
the baseness to lay an honest girl, the most loyal,
the most unselfish of sisters, under contribution to
the same end. Laura crimsoned with the sense that
she had been, unsuspectingly, part of a scheme, that
she was being used as the two women opposite were
used, but that she had been outraged into the bargain, inasmuch as she was not, like them, a conscious
accomplice and not a person to be given away in
that manner before hundreds of people. It came
back to her how bad Selina had been the day of the
business in Lincoln's Inn Fields, and how in spite
of intervening comedies the woman who had then
found such words of injury would be sure to break
out in a new spot with a new weapon. Accordingly,
while the pure music filled the place and the rich
picture of the stage glowed beneath it, Laura found
herself face to face with the strange inference that
the evil of Selina's nature made her wish—since she
had given herself to it—to bring her sister to her
own colour by putting an appearance of 'fastness'

upon her. The girl said to herself that she would
have succeeded, in the cynical view of London ; and
to her troubled spirit the immense theatre had a
myriad eyes, eyes that she knew, eyes that would
know her, that would see her sitting there with a
strange young man. She had recognised many
faces already and her imagination quickly multiplied
them. However, after she had burned a while with
this particular revolt she ceased to think of herself
and of what, as regarded herself, Selina had intended : all her thought went to the mere calculation
of Mrs. Berrington's return. As she did not return,
and still did not, Laura felt a sharp constriction of
the heart. She knew not what she feared—she
knew not what she supposed. She was so nervous
(as she had been the night she waited, till morning,
for her sister to re-enter the house in Grosvenor
Place) that when Mr. Wendover occasionally made
a remark to her she failed to understand him, was
unable to answer him. Fortunately he made very
few ; he was preoccupied—either wondering also
what Selina was ' up to ' or, more probably, simply
absorbed in the music. What she *had* comprehended,
however, was that when at three different moments
she had said, restlessly, ' Why doesn't Mr. Booker
come back ? ' he replied, ' Oh, there's plenty of time
—we are very comfortable.' These words she was
conscious of ; she particularly noted them and they
interwove themselves with her restlessness. She also
noted, in her tension, that after her third inquiry
Mr. Wendover said something about looking up his
friend, if she didn't mind being left alone a moment.
He quitted the box and during this interval Laura
tried more than ever to see with her glass what had

become of her sister. But it was as if the ladies opposite had arranged themselves, had arranged their curtains, on purpose to frustrate such an attempt : it was impossible to her even to assure herself of what she had begun to suspect, that Selina was now not with them. If she was not with them where in the world had she gone ? As the moments elapsed, before Mr. Wendover's return, she went to the door of the box and stood watching the lobby, for the chance that he would bring back the absentee. Presently she saw him coming alone, and something in the expression of his face made her step out into the lobby to meet him. He was smiling, but he looked embarrassed and strange, especially when he saw her standing there as if she wished to leave the place.

' I hope you don't want to go,' he said, holding the door for her to pass back into the box.

' Where are they—where are they ? ' she demanded, remaining in the corridor.

' I saw our friend—he has found a place in the stalls, near the door by which you go into them— just here under us.'

' And does he like that better ? '

Mr. Wendover's smile became perfunctory as he looked down at her. ' Mrs. Berrington has made such an amusing request of him.'

' An amusing request ? '

' She made him promise not to come back.'

' Made him promise——? ' Laura stared.

' She asked him—as a particular favour to her— not to join us again. And he said he wouldn't.'

' Ah, the monster ! ' Laura exclaimed, blushing crimson.

'Do you mean poor Mr. Booker?' Mr. Wendover asked. 'Of course he had to assure her that the wish of so lovely a lady was law. But he doesn't understand!' laughed the young man.

'No more do I. And where is the lovely lady?' said Laura, trying to recover herself.

'He hasn't the least idea.'

'Isn't she with Lady Ringrose?'

'If you like I will go and see.'

Laura hesitated, looking down the curved lobby, where there was nothing to see but the little numbered doors of the boxes. They were alone in the lamplit bareness; the *finale* of the act was ringing and booming behind them. In a moment she said: 'I'm afraid I must trouble you to put me into a cab.'

'Ah, you won't see the rest? *Do* stay—what difference does it make?' And her companion still held open the door of the box. Her eyes met his, in which it seemed to her that as well as in his voice there was conscious sympathy, entreaty, vindication, tenderness. Then she gazed into the vulgar corridor again; something said to her that if she should return she would be taking the most important step of her life. She considered this, and while she did so a great burst of applause filled the place as the curtain fell. 'See what we are losing! And the last act is so fine,' said Mr. Wendover. She returned to her seat and he closed the door of the box behind them.

Then, in this little upholstered receptacle which was so public and yet so private, Laura Wing passed through the strangest moments she had known. An indication of their strangeness is that when she pre-

sently perceived that while she was in the lobby
Lady Ringrose and her companion had quite disappeared, she observed the circumstance without an
exclamation, holding herself silent.   Their box was
empty, but Laura looked at it without in the least
feeling this to be a sign that Selina would now come
round.   She would never come round again, nor
would she have gone home from the opera.   That
was by this time absolutely definite to the girl, who
had first been hot and now was cold with the sense
of what Selina's injunction to poor Mr. Booker
exactly meant.   It was worthy of her, for it was
simply a vicious little kick as she took her flight.
Grosvenor Place would not shelter her that night
and would never shelter her more : that was the
reason she tried to spatter her sister with the mud
into which she herself had jumped.   She would not
have dared to treat her in such a fashion if they had
had a prospect of meeting again.   The strangest
part of this remarkable juncture was that what
ministered most to our young lady's suppressed
emotion was not the tremendous reflection that this
time Selina had really 'bolted' and that on the
morrow all London would know it : all that had
taken the glare of certainty (and a very hideous hue
it was), whereas the chill that had fallen upon the
girl now was that of a mystery which waited to be
cleared up.   Her heart was full of suspense—suspense of which she returned the pressure, trying to
twist it into expectation.   There was a certain
chance in life that sat there beside her, but it would
go for ever if it should not move nearer that night ;
and she listened, she watched, for it to move.   I
need not inform the reader that this chance presented

itself in the person of Mr. Wendover, who more than
any one she knew had it in his hand to transmute
her detestable position.   To-morrow he would know,
and would think sufficiently little of a young person
of *that* breed : therefore it could only be a question
of his speaking on the spot.   That was what she
had come back into the box for—to give him his
opportunity.   It was open to her to think he had
asked for it—adding everything together.

The poor girl added, added, deep in her heart,
while she said nothing.   The music was not there
now, to keep them silent ; yet he remained quiet,
even as she did, and that for some minutes was a
part of her addition.   She felt as if she were running
a race with failure and shame ; she would get in
first if she should get in before the degradation of
the morrow.   But this was not very far off, and
every minute brought it nearer.   It would be there
in fact, virtually, that night, if Mr. Wendover should
begin to realise the brutality of Selina's not turning
up at all.   The comfort had been, hitherto, that he
didn't realise brutalities.   There were certain violins
that emitted tentative sounds in the orchestra ; they
shortened the time and made her uneasier—fixed
her idea that he could lift her out of her mire if he
would.   It didn't appear to prove that he would, his
also observing Lady Ringrose's empty box without
making an encouraging comment upon it.   Laura
waited for him to remark that her sister obviously
would turn up now ; but no such words fell from
his lips.   He must either like Selina's being away or
judge it damningly, and in either case why didn't he
speak ?   If he had nothing to say, why *had* he said,
why had he done, what did he mean——?   But the

girl's inward challenge to him lost itself in a mist of
faintness; she was screwing herself up to a purpose
of her own, and it hurt almost to anguish, and the
whole place, around her, was a blur and swim,
through which she heard the tuning of fiddles.
Before she knew it she had said to him, ' Why have
you come so often ? '

' So often ?   To see you, do you mean ? '

' To see *me*—it was for that ?   Why have you
come ? ' she went on.   He was evidently surprised,
and his surprise gave her a point of anger, a desire
almost that her words should hurt him, lash him.
She spoke low, but she heard herself, and she
thought that if what she said sounded to *him* in the
same way——!   ' You have come very often—too
often, too often ! '

He coloured, he looked frightened, he was, clearly,
extremely startled.   ' Why, you have been so kind,
so delightful,' he stammered.

' Yes, of course, and so have you !   Did you come
for Selina ?   She is married, you know, and devoted
to her husband.'   A single minute had sufficed to
show the girl that her companion was quite un-
prepared for her question, that he was distinctly not
in love with her and was face to face with a situation
entirely new.   The effect of this perception was to
make her say wilder things.

' Why, what is more natural, when one likes
people, than to come often ?   Perhaps I have bored
you—with our American way,' said Mr. Wendover.

' And is it because you like me that you have
kept me here ? ' Laura asked.   She got up, leaning
against the side of the box ; she had pulled the
curtain far forward and was out of sight of the house.

He rose, but more slowly; he had got over his first confusion. He smiled at her, but his smile was dreadful. 'Can you have any doubt as to what I have come for? It's a pleasure to me that you have liked me well enough to ask.'

For an instant she thought he was coming nearer to her, but he didn't: he stood there twirling his gloves. Then an unspeakable shame and horror— horror of herself, of him, of everything—came over her, and she sank into a chair at the back of the box, with averted eyes, trying to get further into her corner. 'Leave me, leave me, go away!' she said, in the lowest tone that he could hear. The whole house seemed to her to be listening to her, pressing into the box.

'Leave you alone—in this place—when I love you? I can't do that—indeed I can't.'

'You don't love me—and you torture me by staying!' Laura went on, in a convulsed voice. 'For God's sake go away and don't speak to me, don't let me see you or hear of you again!'

Mr. Wendover still stood there, exceedingly agitated, as well he might be, by this inconceivable scene. Unaccustomed feelings possessed him and they moved him in different directions. Her command that he should take himself off was passionate, yet he attempted to resist, to speak. How would she get home—would she see him to-morrow—would she let him wait for her outside? To this Laura only replied: 'Oh dear, oh dear, if you would only go!' and at the same instant she sprang up, gathering her cloak around her as if to escape from him, to rush away herself. He checked this movement, however, clapping on his hat and holding the door. One

moment more he looked at her—her own eyes were
closed ; then he exclaimed, pitifully, ' Oh Miss Wing,
oh Miss Wing ! ' and stepped out of the box.

When he had gone she collapsed into one of the
chairs again and sat there with her face buried in
a fold of her mantle.   For many minutes she was
perfectly still — she was ashamed even to move.
The one thing that could have justified her, blown
away the dishonour of her monstrous overture, would
have been, on his side, the quick response of unmis-
takable passion.   It had not come, and she had
nothing left but to loathe herself.   She did so,
violently, for a long time, in the dark corner of the
box, and she felt that he loathed her too.   ' I love
you!'—how pitifully the poor little make-believe words
had quavered out and how much disgust they must
have represented !   ' Poor man—poor man ! ' Laura
Wing suddenly found herself murmuring : compas-
sion filled her mind at the sense of the way she had
used him.   At the same moment a flare of music
broke out : the last act of the opera had begun and
she had sprung up and quitted the box.

The passages were empty and she made her way
without trouble.   She descended to the vestibule ;
there was no one to stare at her and her only fear
was that Mr. Wendover would be there.   But he was
not, apparently, and she saw that she should be able
to go away quickly.   Selina would have taken the
carriage—she could be sure of that ; or if she hadn't
it wouldn't have come back yet ; besides, she couldn't
possibly wait there so long as while it was called.
She was in the act of asking one of the attendants,
in the portico, to get her a cab, when some one
hurried up to her from behind, overtaking her—a

gentleman in whom, turning round, she recognised
Mr. Booker. He looked almost as bewildered as
Mr. Wendover, and his appearance disconcerted her
almost as much as that of his friend would have
done. 'Oh, are you going away, alone? What
must you think of me?' this young man exclaimed;
and he began to tell her something about her sister
and to ask her at the same time if he might not go
with her—help her in some way. He made no
inquiry about Mr. Wendover, and she afterwards
judged that that distracted gentleman had sought
him out and sent him to her assistance; also that he
himself was at that moment watching them from
behind some column. He would have been hateful
if he had shown himself; yet (in this later medita-
tion) there was a voice in her heart which commended
his delicacy. He effaced himself to look after her—
he provided for her departure by proxy.

'A cab, a cab—that's all I want!' she said to
Mr. Booker; and she almost pushed him out of the
place with the wave of the hand with which she
indicated her need. He rushed off to call one, and
a minute afterwards the messenger whom she had
already despatched rattled up in a hansom. She
quickly got into it, and as she rolled away she saw
Mr. Booker returning in all haste with another. She
gave a passionate moan—this common confusion
seemed to add a grotesqueness to her predicament.

XII

THE next day, at five o'clock, she drove to Queen's
Gate, turning to Lady Davenant in her distress in
order to turn somewhere. Her old friend was at
home and by extreme good fortune alone ; looking
up from her book, in her place by the window, she
gave the girl as she came in a sharp glance over
her glasses. This glance was acquisitive ; she said
nothing, but laying down her book stretched out her
two gloved hands. Laura took them and she drew
her down toward her, so that the girl sunk on her
knees and in a moment hid her face, sobbing, in the
old woman's lap. There was nothing said for some
time : Lady Davenant only pressed her tenderly—
stroked her with her hands. 'Is it very bad ?' she
asked at last. Then Laura got up, saying as she
took a seat, 'Have you heard of it and do people
know it ?'

'I haven't heard anything. Is it very bad ?'
Lady Davenant repeated.

'We don't know where Selina is—and her maid's
gone.'

Lady Davenant looked at her visitor a moment.
'Lord, what an ass !' she then ejaculated, putting
the paper-knife into her book to keep her place.

'And whom has she persuaded to take her—Charles
Crispin?' she added.

'We suppose—we suppose——' said Laura.

'And he's another,' interrupted the old woman.
And who supposes—Geordie and Ferdy?'

'I don't know; it's all black darkness!'

'My dear, it's a blessing, and now you can live in
peace.'

'In peace!' cried Laura; 'with my wretched sister
leading such a life?'

'Oh, my dear, I daresay it will be very comfortable; I am sorry to say anything in favour of
such doings, but it very often is.   Don't worry; you
take her too hard.   Has she gone abroad?' the old
lady continued.   'I daresay she has gone to some
pretty, amusing place.'

'I don't know anything about it.   I only know
she is gone.   I was with her last evening and she
left me without a word.'

'Well, that was better.   I hate 'em when they
make parting scenes: it's too mawkish!'

'Lionel has people watching them,' said the girl;
'agents, detectives, I don't know what.   He has had
them for a long time; I didn't know it.'

'Do you mean you would have told her if you
had?   What is the use of detectives now?   Isn't he
rid of her?'

'Oh, I don't know, he's as bad as she; he talks
too horribly—he wants every one to know it,' Laura
groaned.

'And has he told his mother?'

'I suppose so: he rushed off to see her at noon.
She'll be overwhelmed.'

'Overwhelmed?   Not a bit of it!' cried Lady

Davenant, almost gaily. 'When did anything in the world overwhelm her and what do you take her for? She'll only make some delightful odd speech. As for people knowing it,' she added, 'they'll know it whether he wants them or not. My poor child, how long do you expect to make believe?'

'Lionel expects some news to-night,' Laura said. 'As soon as I know where she is I shall start.'

'Start for where?'

'To go to her—to do something.'

'Something preposterous, my dear. Do you expect to bring her back?'

'He won't take her in,' said Laura, with her dried, dismal eyes. 'He wants his divorce—it's too hideous!'

'Well, as she wants hers what is simpler?'

'Yes, she wants hers. Lionel swears by all the gods she can't get it.'

'Bless me, won't one do?' Lady Davenant asked. 'We shall have some pretty reading.'

'It's awful, awful, awful!' murmured Laura.

'Yes, they oughtn't to be allowed to publish them. I wonder if we couldn't stop that. At any rate he had better be quiet: tell him to come and see me.'

'You won't influence him; he's dreadful against her. Such a house as it is to-day!'

'Well, my dear, naturally.'

'Yes, but it's terrible for me: it's all more sickening than I can bear.'

'My dear child, come and stay with me,' said the old woman, gently.

'Oh, I can't desert her; I can't abandon her!'

'Desert—abandon? What a way to put it! Hasn't she abandoned you?'

'She has no heart—she's too base!' said the girl. Her face was white and the tears now began to rise to her eyes again.

Lady Davenant got up and came and sat on the sofa beside her : she put her arms round her and the two women embraced. 'Your room is all ready,' the old lady remarked. And then she said, 'When did she leave you? When did you see her last?'

'Oh, in the strangest, maddest, cruelest way, the way most insulting to me. We went to the opera together and she left me there with a gentleman. We know nothing about her since.'

'With a gentleman?'

'With Mr. Wendover—that American, and something too dreadful happened.'

'Dear me, did he kiss you?' asked Lady Davenant.

Laura got up quickly, turning away. 'Good-bye, I'm going, I'm going!' And in reply to an irritated, protesting exclamation from her companion she went on, 'Anywhere—anywhere to get away!'

'To get away from your American?'

'I asked him to marry me!' The girl turned round with her tragic face.

'He oughtn't to have left that to you.'

'I knew this horror was coming and it took possession of me, there in the box, from one moment to the other—the idea of making sure of some other life, some protection, some respectability. First I thought he liked me, he had behaved as if he did. And I like him, he is a very good man. So I asked him, I couldn't help it, it was too hideous—I offered

myself!' Laura spoke as if she were telling that
she had stabbed him, standing there with dilated
eyes.

Lady Davenant got up again and went to her;
drawing off her glove she felt her cheek with the
back of her hand. 'You are ill, you are in a fever.
I'm sure that whatever you said it was very
charming.'

'Yes, I am ill,' said Laura.

'Upon my honour you shan't go home, you shall
go straight to bed. And what did he say to you?'

'Oh, it was too miserable!' cried the girl, pressing her face again into her companion's kerchief.
'I was all, all mistaken; he had never thought!'

'Why the deuce then did he run about that way
after you? He was a brute to say it!'

'He didn't say it and he never ran about. He
behaved like a perfect gentleman.'

'I've no patience—I wish I had seen him that
time!' Lady Davenant declared.

'Yes, that would have been nice! You'll never
see him; if he *is* a gentleman he'll rush away.'

'Bless me, what a rushing away!' murmured the
old woman. Then passing her arm round Laura
she added, 'You'll please to come upstairs with
me.'

Half an hour later she had some conversation
with her butler which led to his consulting a little
register into which it was his law to transcribe with
great neatness, from their cards, the addresses of
new visitors. This volume, kept in the drawer of
the hall table, revealed the fact that Mr. Wendover
was staying in George Street, Hanover Square.
'Get into a cab immediately and tell him to come

and see me this evening,' Lady Davenant said.
'Make him understand that it interests him very
nearly, so that no matter what his engagements may
be he must give them up. Go quickly and you'll
just find him : he'll be sure to be at home to dress
for dinner.' She had calculated justly, for a few
minutes before ten o'clock the door of her drawing-
room was thrown open and Mr. Wendover was
announced.

  'Sit there,' said the old lady ; 'no, not that one,
nearer to me. We must talk low. My dear sir, I
won't bite you !'

  'Oh, this is very comfortable,' Mr. Wendover
replied vaguely, smiling through his visible anxiety.
It was no more than natural that he should wonder
what Laura Wing's peremptory friend wanted of
him at that hour of the night ; but nothing could
exceed the gallantry of his attempt to conceal the
symptoms of alarm.

  'You ought to have come before, you know,'
Lady Davenant went on. 'I have wanted to see
you more than once.'

  'I have been dining out—I hurried away. This
was the first possible moment, I assure you.'

  'I too was dining out and I stopped at home on
purpose to see you. But I didn't mean to-night, for
you have done very well. I was quite intending to
send for you—the other day. But something put
it out of my head. Besides, I knew she wouldn't
like it.'

  'Why, Lady Davenant, I made a point of calling,
ever so long ago—after that day !' the young man
exclaimed, not reassured, or at any rate not en-
lightened.

'I daresay you did — but you mustn't justify yourself; that's just what I don't want; it isn't what I sent for you for. I have something very particular to say to you, but it's very difficult. Voyons un peu!'

The old woman reflected a little, with her eyes on his face, which had grown more grave as she went on; its expression intimated that he failed as yet to understand her and that he at least was not exactly trifling. Lady Davenant's musings apparently helped her little, if she was looking for an artful approach; for they ended in her saying abruptly, 'I wonder if you know what a capital girl she is.'

'Do you mean—do you mean——?' stammered Mr. Wendover, pausing as if he had given her no right not to allow him to conceive alternatives.

'Yes, I do mean.   She's upstairs, in bed.'

'Upstairs in bed!'   The young man stared.

'Don't be afraid—I'm not going to send for her!' laughed his hostess; 'her being here, after all, has nothing to do with it, except that she *did* come— yes, certainly, she did come. But my keeping her— that was my doing. My maid has gone to Grosvenor Place to get her things and let them know that she will stay here for the present.   Now am I clear?'

'Not in the least,' said Mr. Wendover, almost sternly.

Lady Davenant, however, was not of a composition to suspect him of sternness or to care very much if she did, and she went on, with her quick discursiveness: 'Well, we must be patient; we shall work it out together.   I was afraid you would go

away, that's why I lost no time.   Above all I want
you to understand that she has not the least idea
that I have sent for you, and you must promise me
never, never, never to let her know.   She would be
monstrous angry.   It is quite my own idea—I have
taken the responsibility.   I know very little about
you of course, but she has spoken to me well of you.
Besides, I am very clever about people, and I liked
you that day, though you seemed to think I was a
hundred and eighty.'

'You do me great honour,' Mr. Wendover rejoined.

'I'm glad you're pleased!   You must be if I tell
you that I like you now even better.   I see what
you are, except for the question of fortune.   It
doesn't perhaps matter much, but have you any
money?   I mean have you a fine income?'

'No, indeed I haven't!'   And the young man
laughed in his bewilderment.   'I have very little
money indeed.'

'Well, I daresay you have as much as I.   Besides, that would be a proof she is not mercenary.'

'You haven't in the least made it plain whom
you are talking about,' said Mr. Wendover.   'I have
no right to assume anything.'

'Are you afraid of betraying her?   I am more
devoted to her even than I want you to be.   She
has told me what happened between you last night
—what she said to you at the opera.   That's what
I want to talk to you about.'

'She was very strange,' the young man remarked.

'I am not so sure that she was strange.   However, you are welcome to think it, for goodness
knows she says so herself.   She is overwhelmed

with horror at her own words ; she is absolutely distracted and prostrate.'

Mr. Wendover was silent a moment.   'I assured her that I admire her—beyond every one.   I was most kind to her.'

'Did you say it in that tone ?   You should have thrown yourself at her feet !   From the moment you didn't—surely you understand women well enough to know.'

'You must remember where we were—in a public place, with very little room for throwing !' Mr. Wendover exclaimed.

'Ah, so far from blaming you she says your behaviour was perfect. It's only I who want to have it out with you,' Lady Davenant pursued. 'She's so clever, so charming, so good and so unhappy.'

'When I said just now she was strange, I meant only in the way she turned against me.'

'She turned against you ?'

'She told me she hoped she should never see me again.'

'And you, should you like to see her ?'

'Not now—not now !' Mr. Wendover exclaimed, eagerly.

'I don't mean now, I'm not such a fool as that. I mean some day or other, when she has stopped accusing herself, if she ever does.'

'Ah, Lady Davenant, you must leave that to me,' the young man returned, after a moment's hesitation.

'Don't be afraid to tell me I'm meddling with what doesn't concern me,' said his hostess. 'Of course I know I'm meddling ; I sent for you here to meddle.   Who wouldn't, for that creature ?   She makes one melt.'

'I'm exceedingly sorry for her. I don't know what she thinks she said.'

'Well, that she asked you why you came so often to Grosvenor Place. I don't see anything so awful in that, if you did go.'

'Yes, I went very often. I liked to go.'

'Now, that's exactly where I wish to prevent a misconception,' said Lady Davenant. 'If you liked to go you had a reason for liking, and Laura Wing was the reason, wasn't she?'

'I thought her charming, and I think her so now more than ever.'

'Then you are a dear good man. Vous faisiez votre cour, in short.'

Mr. Wendover made no immediate response: the two sat looking at each other. 'It isn't easy for me to talk of these things,' he said at last; 'but if you mean that I wished to ask her to be my wife I am bound to tell you that I had no such intention.'

'Ah, then I'm at sea. You thought her charming and you went to see her every day. What then did you wish?'

'I didn't go every day. Moreover I think you have a very different idea in this country of what constitutes—well, what constitutes making love. A man commits himself much sooner.'

'Oh, I don't know what *your* odd ways may be!' Lady Davenant exclaimed, with a shade of irritation.

'Yes, but I was justified in supposing that those ladies did: they at least are American.'

'"They," my dear sir! For heaven's sake don't mix up that nasty Selina with it!'

'Why not, if I admired her too? I do extremely, and I thought the house most interesting.'

'Mercy on us, if that's your idea of a nice house!
But I don't know——I have always kept out of it,'
Lady Davenant added, checking herself.   Then she
went on, 'If you are so fond of Mrs. Berrington I
am sorry to inform you that she is absolutely good-
for-nothing.'

'Good-for-nothing?'

'Nothing to speak of!   I have been thinking
whether I would tell you, and I have decided to do
so because I take it that your learning it for yourself would be a matter of but a very short time.
Selina has bolted, as they say.'

'Bolted?' Mr. Wendover repeated.

'I don't know what you call it in America.'

'In America we don't do it.'

'Ah, well, if they stay, as they do usually abroad,
that's better.   I suppose you didn't think her capable
of behaving herself, did you?'

'Do you mean she has left her husband——with
some one else?'

'Neither more nor less; with a fellow named
Crispin.   It appears it all came off last evening, and
she had her own reasons for doing it in the most
offensive way——publicly, clumsily, with the vulgarest
bravado.   Laura has told me what took place, and
you must permit me to express my surprise at your
not having divined the miserable business.'

'I saw something was wrong, but I didn't understand.   I'm afraid I'm not very quick at these things.'

'Your state is the more gracious; but certainly
you are not quick if you could call there so often
and not see through Selina.'

'Mr. Crispin, whoever he is, was never there,'
said the young man.

'Oh, she was a clever hussy!' his companion rejoined.

'I knew she was fond of amusement, but that's what I liked to see. I wanted to see a house of that sort.'

'Fond of amusement is a very pretty phrase!' said Lady Davenant, laughing at the simplicity with which her visitor accounted for his assiduity. 'And did Laura Wing seem to you in her place in a house of that sort?'

'Why, it was natural she should be with her sister, and she always struck me as very gay.'

'That was your enlivening effect! And did she strike you as very gay last night, with this scandal hanging over her?'

'She didn't talk much,' said Mr. Wendover.

'She knew it was coming—she felt it, she saw it, and that's what makes her sick now, that at *such* a time she should have challenged you, when she felt herself about to be associated (in people's minds, of course) with such a vile business. In people's minds and in yours—when you should know what had happened.'

'Ah, Miss Wing isn't associated——' said Mr. Wendover. He spoke slowly, but he rose to his feet with a nervous movement that was not lost upon his companion: she noted it indeed with a certain inward sense of triumph. She was very deep, but she had never been so deep as when she made up her mind to mention the scandal of the house of Berrington to her visitor and intimated to him that Laura Wing regarded herself as near enough to it to receive from it a personal stain. 'I'm extremely sorry to hear of Mrs. Berrington's misconduct,' he continued gravely, standing before her. 'And I am no less obliged to you for your interest.'

'Don't mention it,' she said, getting up too and smiling. 'I mean my interest. As for the other matter, it will all come out. Lionel will haul her up.'

'Dear me, how dreadful!'

'Yes, dreadful enough. But don't betray me.'

'Betray you?' he repeated, as if his thoughts had gone astray a moment.

'I mean to the girl. Think of her shame!'

'Her shame?' Mr. Wendover said, in the same way.

'It seemed to her, with what was becoming so clear to her, that an honest man might save her from it, might give her his name and his faith and help her to traverse the bad place. She exaggerates the badness of it, the stigma of her relationship. Good heavens, at that rate where would some of us be? But those are her ideas, they are absolutely sincere, and they had possession of her at the opera. She had a sense of being lost and was in a real agony to be rescued. She saw before her a kind gentleman who had seemed—who had certainly seemed——' And Lady Davenant, with her fine old face lighted by her bright sagacity and her eyes on Mr. Wendover's, paused, lingering on this word. 'Of course she must have been in a state of nerves.'

'I am very sorry for her,' said Mr. Wendover, with his gravity that committed him to nothing.

'So am I! And of course if you were not in love with her you weren't, were you?'

'I must bid you good-bye, I am leaving London.'

That was the only answer Lady Davenant got to her inquiry.

'Good-bye then.   She is the nicest girl I know. But once more, mind you don't let her suspect!'

'How can I let her suspect anything when I shall never see her again?'

'Oh, don't say that,' said Lady Davenant, very gently.

'She drove me away from her with a kind of ferocity.'

'Oh, gammon!' cried the old woman.

'I'm going home,' he said, looking at her with his hand on the door.

'Well, it's the best place for you.   And for her too!' she added as he went out.   She was not sure that the last words reached him.

XIII

LAURA WING was sharply ill for three days, but on the fourth she made up her mind she was better, though this was not the opinion of Lady Davenant, who would not hear of her getting up. The remedy she urged was lying still and yet lying still ; but this specific the girl found well-nigh intolerable—it was a form of relief that only ministered to fever. She assured her friend that it killed her to do nothing : to which her friend replied by asking her what she had a fancy to do. Laura had her idea and held it tight, but there was no use in producing it before Lady Davenant, who would have knocked it to pieces. On the afternoon of the first day Lionel Berrington came, and though his intention was honest he brought no healing. Hearing she was ill he wanted to look after her—he wanted to take her back to Grosvenor Place and make her comfortable : he spoke as if he had every convenience for producing that condition, though he confessed there was a little bar to it in his own case. This impediment was the 'cheeky' aspect of Miss Steet, who went sniffing about as if she knew a lot, if she should only condescend to tell it. He saw more of the children now ; ' I'm going to have 'em in every day, poor little

devils,' h[,] said ; and he spoke as if the discipline
of suffering had already begun for him and a kind of
holy change had taken place in his life.   Nothing
had been said yet in the house, of course, as Laura
knew, about Selina's disappearance, in the way of
treating it as irregular ; but the servants pretended
so hard not to be aware of anything in particular
that they were like pickpockets looking with un-
natural interest the other way after they have cribbed
a fellow's watch.   To a certainty, in a day or two,
the governess would give him warning : she would
come and tell him she couldn't stay in such a place,
and he would tell her, in return, that she was a little
donkey for not knowing that the place was much
more respectable now than it had ever been.

This information Selina's husband imparted to
Lady Davenant, to whom he discoursed with infinite
candour and humour, taking a highly philosophical
view of his position and declaring that it suited him
down to the ground.   His wife couldn't have pleased
him better if she had done it on purpose ; he knew
where she had been every hour since she quitted
Laura at the opera—he knew where she was at that
moment and he was expecting to find another tele-
gram on his return to Grosvenor Place.   So if it
suited *her* it was all right, wasn't it? and the whole
thing would go as straight as a shot.   Lady Davenant took him up to see Laura, though she viewed
their meeting with extreme disfavour, the girl being
in no state for talking.   In general Laura had little
enough mind for it, but she insisted on seeing Lionel :
she declared that if this were not allowed her she
would go after him, ill as she was—she would dress
herself and drive to his house.   She dressed herself

now, after a fashion ; she got upon a sofa to receive
him.   Lady Davenant left him alone with her for
twenty minutes, at the end of which she returned to
take him away.   This interview was not fortifying
to the girl, whose idea—the idea of which I have
said that she was tenacious—was to go after her
sister, to take possession of her, cling to her and
bring her back.   Lionel, of course, wouldn't hear of
taking her back, nor would Selina presumably hear
of coming ; but this made no difference in Laura's
heroic plan.   She would work it, she would compass
it, she would go down on her knees, she would find
the eloquence of angels, she would achieve miracles.
At any rate it made her frantic not to try, especially
as even in fruitless action she should escape from
herself—an object of which her horror was not yet
extinguished.

As she lay there through inexorably conscious
hours the picture of that hideous moment in the
box alternated with the vision of her sister's guilty
flight.   She wanted to fly, herself—to go off and
keep going for ever.   Lionel was fussily kind to
her and he didn't abuse Selina—he didn't tell her
again how that lady's behaviour suited his book.   He
simply resisted, with a little exasperating, dogged
grin, her pitiful appeal for knowledge of her sister's
whereabouts.   He knew what she wanted it for and
he wouldn't help her in any such game.   If she
would promise, solemnly, to be quiet, he would tell
her when she got better, but he wouldn't lend her a
hand to make a fool of herself.   Her work was cut
out for her—she was to stay and mind the children :
if she was so keen to do her duty she needn't go
further than that for it.   He talked a great deal

about the children and figured himself as pressing the little deserted darlings to his bosom. He was not a comedian, and she could see that he really believed he was going to be better and purer now. Laura said she was sure Selina would make an attempt to get them—or at least one of them ; and he replied, grimly, ' Yes, my dear, she had better try ! ' The girl was so angry with him, in her hot, tossing weakness, for refusing to tell her even whether the desperate pair had crossed the Channel, that she was guilty of the immorality of regretting that the difference in badness between husband and wife was so distinct (for it was distinct, she could see that) as he made his dry little remark about Selina's trying. He told her he had already seen his solicitor, the clever Mr. Smallshaw, and she said she didn't care.

On the fourth day of her absence from Grosvenor Place she got up, at an hour when she was alone (in the afternoon, rather late), and prepared herself to go out. Lady Davenant had admitted in the morning that she was better, and fortunately she had not the complication of being subject to a medical opinion, having absolutely refused to see a doctor. Her old friend had been obliged to go out—she had scarcely quitted her before—and Laura had requested the hovering, rustling lady's-maid to leave her alone : she assured her she was doing beautifully. Laura had no plan except to leave London that night ; she had a moral certainty that Selina had gone to the Continent. She had always done so whenever she had a chance, and what chance had ever been larger than the present ? The Continent was fearfully vague, but she would deal sharply with Lionel —she would show him she had a right to knowledge.

He would certainly be in town ; he would be in a
complacent bustle with his lawyers. She had told
him that she didn't believe he had yet gone to them,
but in her heart she believed it perfectly. If he
didn't satisfy her she would go to Lady Ringrose,
odious as it would be to her to ask a favour of this
depraved creature : unless indeed Lady Ringrose
had joined the little party to France, as on the
occasion of Selina's last journey thither. On her
way downstairs she met one of the footmen, of whom
she made the request that he would call her a cab
as quickly as possible—she was obliged to go out
for half an hour. He expressed the respectful hope
that she was better and she replied that she was
perfectly well—he would please tell her ladyship
when she came in. To this the footman rejoined
that her ladyship *had* come in—she had returned
five minutes before and had gone to her room.
' Miss Frothingham told her you were asleep, Miss,'
said the man, ' and her ladyship said it was a blessing and you were not to be disturbed.'

'Very good, I will see her,' Laura remarked, with
dissimulation : ' only please let me have my cab.'

The footman went downstairs and she stood
there listening ; presently she heard the house-door
close—he had gone out on his errand. Then she
descended very softly—she prayed he might not be
long. The door of the drawing-room stood open as
she passed it, and she paused before it, thinking she
heard sounds in the lower hall. They appeared to
subside and then she found herself faint—she was
terribly impatient for her cab. Partly to sit down
till it came (there was a seat on the landing, but
another servant might come up or down and see

her), and partly to look, at the front window, whether
it were not coming, she went for a moment into the
drawing-room.　She stood at the window, but the
footman was slow ; then she sank upon a chair—
she felt very weak.　Just after she had done so she
became aware of steps on the stairs and she got up
quickly, supposing that her messenger had returned,
though she had not heard wheels.　What she saw
was not the footman she had sent out, but the ex-
pansive person of the butler, followed apparently by a
visitor.　This functionary ushered the visitor in with
the remark that he would call her ladyship, and
before she knew it she was face to face with Mr.
Wendover.　At the same moment she heard a cab
drive up, while Mr. Wendover instantly closed the door.

'Don't turn me away ; do see me—do see me !'
he said.　'I asked for Lady Davenant—they told
me she was at home.　But it was you I wanted,
and I wanted her to help me.　I was going away—
but I couldn't.　You look very ill—do listen to me !
You don't understand—I will explain everything.
Ah, how ill you look !' the young man cried, as
the climax of this sudden, soft, distressed appeal.
Laura, for all answer, tried to push past him, but
the result of this movement was that she found herself enclosed in his arms.　He stopped her, but she
disengaged herself, she got her hand upon the door.
He was leaning against it, so she couldn't open it,
and as she stood there panting she shut her eyes, so
as not to see him.　'If you would let me tell you
what I think—I would do anything in the world for
you !' he went on.

'Let me go—you persecute me !' the girl cried,
pulling at the handle.

'You don't do me justice—you are too cruel!'
Mr. Wendover persisted.

'Let me go—let me go!' she only repeated,
with her high, quavering, distracted note; and as
he moved a little she got the door open. But he
followed her out: would she see him that night?
Where was she going? might he not go with her?
would she see him to-morrow?

'Never, never, never!' she flung at him as she
hurried away. The butler was on the stairs, de-
scending from above; so he checked himself, letting
her go. Laura passed out of the house and flew
into her cab with extraordinary speed, for Mr.
Wendover heard the wheels bear her away while
the servant was saying to him in measured accents
that her ladyship would come down immediately.

Lionel was at home, in Grosvenor Place: she
burst into the library and found him playing papa.
Geordie and Ferdy were sporting around him, the
presence of Miss Steet had been dispensed with, and
he was holding his younger son by the stomach,
horizontally, between his legs, while the child made
little sprawling movements which were apparently
intended to represent the act of swimming. Geordie
stood impatient on the brink of the imaginary stream,
protesting that it was his turn now, and as soon as
he saw his aunt he rushed at her with the request
that she would take him up in the same fashion.
She was struck with the superficiality of their childhood; they appeared to have no sense that she had
been away and no care that she had been ill. But
Lionel made up for this; he greeted her with affec-
tionate jollity, said it was a good job she had come
back, and remarked to the children that they would

have great larks now that auntie was home again.
Ferdy asked if she had been with mummy, but didn't
wait for an answer, and she observed that they put
no question about their mother and made no further
allusion to her while they remained in the room.
She wondered whether their father had enjoined
upon them not to mention her, and reflected that
even if he had such a command would not have
been efficacious. It added to the ugliness of Selina's
flight that even her children didn't miss her, and to
the dreariness, somehow, to Laura's sense, of the
whole situation that one could neither spend tears
on the mother and wife, because she was not worth
it, nor sentimentalise about the little boys, because
they didn't inspire it. 'Well, you do look seedy—
I'm bound to say that!' Lionel exclaimed; and he
recommended strongly a glass of port, while Ferdy,
not seizing this reference, suggested that daddy
should take her by the waistband and teach her to
'strike out.' He represented himself in the act of
drowning, but Laura interrupted this entertainment,
when the servant answered the bell (Lionel having
rung for the port), by requesting that the children
should be conveyed to Miss Steet. 'Tell her she
must never go away again,' Lionel said to Geordie,
as the butler took him by the hand; but the only
touching consequence of this injunction was that the
child piped back to his father, over his shoulder,
'Well, you mustn't either, you know!'

'You must tell me or I'll kill myself—I give you
my word!' Laura said to her brother-in-law, with
unnecessary violence, as soon as they had left the
room.

'I say, I say,' he rejoined, 'you *are* a wilful one!

What do you want to threaten me for ? Don't you know me well enough to know that ain't the way ? That's the tone Selina used to take. Surely you don't want to begin and imitate her ! ' She only sat there, looking at him, while he leaned against the chimney-piece smoking a short cigar. There was a silence, during which she felt the heat of a certain irrational anger at the thought that a little ignorant, red-faced jockey should have the luck to be in the right as against her flesh and blood. She considered him helplessly, with something in her eyes that had never been there before—something that, apparently, after a moment, made an impression on him. Afterwards, however, she saw very well that it was not her threat that had moved him, and even at the moment she had a sense, from the way he looked back at her, that this was in no manner the first time a baffled woman had told him that she would kill herself. He had always accepted his kinship with her, but even in her trouble it was part of her consciousness that he now lumped her with a mixed group of female figures, a little wavering and dim, who were associated in his memory with ' scenes,' with importunities and bothers. It is apt to be the disadvantage of women, or occasions of measuring their strength with men, that they may perceive that the man has a larger experience and that they themselves are a part of it. It is doubtless as a provision against such emergencies that nature has opened to them operations of the mind that are independent of experience. Laura felt the dishonour of her race the more that her brother-in-law seemed so gay and bright about it : he had an air of positive prosperity, as if his misfortune had turned into that. It came to her that he really liked the idea of the public *éclaircissement*—the fresh occupation, the bustle and importance and celebrity of it. That was sufficiently incredible, but as she was on the wrong side it was also humiliating. Besides, higher spirits always suggest finer wisdom, and such an attribute on Lionel's part was most humiliating of all. 'I haven't the least objection at present to telling you what you want to know. I shall have made my little arrangements very soon and you will be subpœnaed.'

'Subpœnaed?' the girl repeated, mechanically.

'You will be called as a witness on my side.'

'On your side.'

'Of course you're on my side, ain't you?'

'Can they force me to come?' asked Laura, in answer to this.

'No, they can't force you, if you leave the country.'

'That's exactly what I want to do.'

'That will be idiotic,' said Lionel, 'and very bad for your sister. If you don't help me you ought at least to help her.'

She sat a moment with her eyes on the ground. 'Where is she—where is she?' she then asked.

'They are at Brussels, at the Hôtel de Flandres. They appear to like it very much.'

'Are you telling me the truth?'

'Lord, my dear child, *I* don't lie!' Lionel exclaimed. 'You'll make a jolly mistake if you go to her,' he added. 'If you have seen her with him how can you speak for her?'

'I won't see her with him.'

'That's all very well, but he'll take care of that.

Of course if you're ready for perjury———!' Lionel exclaimed.

'I'm ready for anything.'

'Well, I've been kind to you, my dear,' he continued, smoking, with his chin in the air.

'Certainly you have been kind to me.'

'If you want to defend her you had better keep away from her,' said Lionel. 'Besides for yourself, it won't be the best thing in the world—to be known to have been in it.'

'I don't care about myself,' the girl returned, musingly.

'Don't you care about the children, that you are so ready to throw them over? For you would, my dear, you know. If you go to Brussels you never come back here—you never cross this threshold—you never touch them again !'

Laura appeared to listen to this last declaration, but she made no reply to it; she only exclaimed after a moment, with a certain impatience, 'Oh, the children will do anyway!' Then she added passionately, 'You *won't*, Lionel ; in mercy's name tell me that you won't !'

'I won't what ?'

'Do the awful thing you say.'

'Divorce her ? The devil I won't !'

'Then why do you speak of the children—if you have no pity for them ?'

Lionel stared an instant. 'I thought you said yourself that they would do anyway !'

Laura bent her head, resting it on the back of her hand, on the leathern arm of the sofa. So she remained, while Lionel stood smoking ; but at last, to leave the room, she got up with an effort that was a physical pain. He came to her, to detain her, with a little good intention that had no felicity for her, trying to take her hand persuasively. 'Dear old girl, don't try and behave just as *she* did ! If you'll stay quietly here I won't call you, I give you my honour I won't ; there ! You want to see the doctor —that's the fellow you want to see. And what good will it do you, even if you bring her home in pink paper ? Do you candidly suppose I'll ever look at her—except across the court-room ? '

'I must, I must, I must !' Laura cried, jerking herself away from him and reaching the door.

'Well then, good-bye,' he said, in the sternest tone she had ever heard him use.

She made no answer, she only escaped. She locked herself in her room ; she remained there an hour. At the end of this time she came out and went to the door of the schoolroom, where she asked Miss Steet to be so good as to come and speak to her. The governess followed her to her apartment and there Laura took her partly into her confidence. There were things she wanted to do before going, and she was too weak to act without assistance. She didn't want it from the servants, if only Miss Steet would learn from them whether Mr. Berrington were dining at home. Laura told her that her sister was ill and she was hurrying to join her abroad. It had to be mentioned, that way, that Mrs. Berrington had left the country, though of course there was no spoken recognition between the two women of the reasons for which she had done so. There was only a tacit hypocritical assumption that she was on a visit to friends and that there had been nothing queer about her departure. Laura knew that Miss

Steet knew the truth, and the governess knew that
she knew it. This young woman lent a hand, very
confusedly, to the girl's preparations; she ventured
not to be sympathetic, as that would point too much
to badness, but she succeeded perfectly in being
dismal. She suggested that Laura was ill herself,
but Laura replied that this was no matter when her
sister was so much worse. She elicited the fact that
Mr. Berrington was dining out—the butler believed
with his mother—but she was of no use when it
came to finding in the 'Bradshaw' which she
brought up from the hall the hour of the night-boat
to Ostend. Laura found it herself; it was con-
veniently late, and it was a gain to her that she was
very near the Victoria station, where she would take
the train for Dover. The governess wanted to go
to the station with her, but the girl would not listen
to this—she would only allow her to see that she
had a cab. Laura let her help her still further; she
sent her down to talk to Lady Davenant's maid
when that personage arrived in Grosvenor Place to
inquire, from her mistress, what in the world had
become of poor Miss Wing. The maid intimated,
Miss Steet said on her return, that her ladyship
would have come herself, only she was too angry
She was very bad indeed. It was an indication
of this that she had sent back her young friend's
dressing-case and her clothes. Laura also borrowed
money from the governess—she had too little in her
pocket. The latter brightened up as the preparations advanced; she had never before been concerned in a flurried night-episode, with an unavowed
clandestine side; the very imprudence of it (for a
sick girl alone) was romantic, and before Laura had

gone down to the cab she began to say that foreign
life must be fascinating and to make wistful reflections. She saw that the coast was clear, in the
nursery—that the children were asleep, for their
aunt to come in. She kissed Ferdy while her companion pressed her lips upon Geordie, and Geordie
while Laura hung for a moment over Ferdy. At
the door of the cab she tried to make her take
more money, and our heroine had an odd sense
that if the vehicle had not rolled away she would
have thrust into her hand a keepsake for Captain
Crispin.

A quarter of an hour later Laura sat in the corner
of a railway-carriage, muffled in her cloak (the July
evening was fresh, as it so often is in London—fresh
enough to add to her sombre thoughts the suggestion
of the wind in the Channel), waiting in a vain torment
of nervousness for the train to set itself in motion.
Her nervousness itself had led her to come too
early to the station, and it seemed to her that she had
already waited long. A lady and a gentleman had
taken their place in the carriage (it was not yet the
moment for the outward crowd of tourists) and had
left their appurtenances there while they strolled up
and down the platform. The long English twilight
was still in the air, but there was dusk under the
grimy arch of the station and Laura flattered herself
that the off-corner of the carriage she had chosen was
in shadow. This, however, apparently did not prevent
her from being recognised by a gentleman who stopped
at the door, looking in, with the movement of a
person who was going from carriage to carriage.
As soon as he saw her he stepped quickly in, and
the next moment Mr. Wendover was seated on the

edge of the place beside her, leaning toward her,
speaking to her low, with clasped hands. She fell
back in her seat, closing her eyes again. He barred
the way out of the compartment.

'I have followed you here—I saw Miss Steet—
I want to implore you not to go! Don't, don't! I
know what you're doing. Don't go, I beseech you.
I saw Lady Davenant, I wanted to ask her to help
me, I could bear it no longer. I have thought of
you, night and day, these four days. Lady Davenant
has told me things, and I entreat you not to go!'

Laura opened her eyes (there was something in
his voice, in his pressing nearness), and looked at
him a moment : it was the first time she had done
so since the first of those detestable moments in the
box at Covent Garden. She had never spoken to
him of Selina in any but an honourable sense. Now
she said, 'I'm going to my sister.'

'I know it, and I wish unspeakably you would
give it up—it isn't good—it's a great mistake.
Stay here and let me talk to you.'

The girl raised herself, she stood up in the
carriage. Mr. Wendover did the same ; Laura saw
that the lady and gentleman outside were now
standing near the door. 'What have you to say?
It's my own business!' she returned, between her
teeth. 'Go out, go out, go out!'

'Do you suppose I would speak if I didn't care
—do you suppose I would care if I didn't love
you?' the young man murmured, close to her face.

'What is there to care about? Because people
will know it and talk? If it's bad it's the right
thing for me! If I don't go to her where else shall
I go?'

'Come to me, dearest, dearest!' Mr. Wendover went on. 'You are ill, you are mad! I love you —I assure you I do!'

She pushed him away with her hands. 'If you follow me I will jump off the boat!'

'Take your places, take your places!' cried the guard, on the platform. Mr. Wendover had to slip out, the lady and gentleman were coming in. Laura huddled herself into her corner again and presently the train drew away.

Mr. Wendover did not get into another compartment; he went back that evening to Queen's Gate. He knew how interested his old friend there, as he now considered her, would be to hear what Laura had undertaken (though, as he learned, on entering her drawing-room again, she had already heard of it from her maid), and he felt the necessity to tell her once more how her words of four days before had fructified in his heart, what a strange, ineffaceable impression she had made upon him : to tell her in short and to repeat it over and over, that he had taken the most extraordinary fancy——! Lady Davenant was tremendously vexed at the girl's perversity, but she counselled him patience, a long, persistent patience. A week later she heard from Laura Wing, from Antwerp, that she was sailing to America from that port—a letter containing no mention whatever of Selina or of the reception she had found at Brussels. To America Mr. Wendover followed his young compatriot (that at least she had no right to forbid), and there, for the moment, he has had a chance to practise the humble virtue recommended by Lady Davenant. He knows she has no money and that she is staying with some

distant relatives in Virginia; a situation that he—
perhaps too superficially—figures as unspeakably
dreary. He knows further that Lady Davenant has
sent her fifty pounds, and he himself has ideas of
transmitting funds, not directly to Virginia but by
the roundabout road of Queen's Gate. Now, however, that Lionel Berrington's deplorable suit is
coming on he reflects with some satisfaction that the
Court of Probate and Divorce is far from the banks
of the Rappahannock. 'Berrington *versus* Berrington
and Others' is coming on—but these are matters of
the present hour.